AUTHORS NOTES

The events in this book have been recalled to the best of my recollection. All names and some slight details have been changed to protect the identities of individuals involved. With that being said I really hope you enjoy reading about my experiences as much as I did living and writing about them.

This is the story of a Marine that isn't a war hero, he never went to combat, never had to worry about dying or leaving his family behind. This is the Marine that got stationed in Hawaii after the war had come and gone. He showed up to work on time and did his job well, but when the uniform came off and the weekend came he went out to party and did things that he probably should have gotten in trouble for. This is his story…

1. Joining

Sometime in August, during the summer of 2011 before I started my senior year in high school, I was at work cleaning a pool for my father's pool service company. I bent over to empty the basket that collects the dirt and trash off the surface of the water, and for what seemed like the 100th time, I saw a dead animal in the basket. It smelt like rotten milk and made me want to vomit instantly. It was in that moment that I knew I wouldn't be able to clean pools for the rest of my life, It wasn't a career path that I wanted to see through.

The high school that I attended was Palmetto Ridge high school. It was a fairly big school where about 1000 students attended. My graduating class consisted of about 300 students. I was a very average guy, one of those people who were more of an in between guy, I wasn't a complete loser but wasn't one of the popular dudes who played on the shitty football team. I did what the typical high school kids did, I smoked a fuck ton of weed, went to parties to get smashed, and had those awkward teenage sex experiences. As for my grades, well below average is quite the understatement, the requirement to graduate was a 2.0 GPA with around 28 credits, and my final GPA was a 2.0001. Instead of studying for my classes to get good grades, I decided that I would make just enough effort to graduate doing as little as I possibly could and skipping classes when I knew it wouldn't hurt me. If I would have just studied for my classes, I probably could have gotten decent grades and I might have had a different future than the one that I chose.

Anyway, this story isn't supposed to be about my high school experience, this is about my enlistment. Getting back to that, after I determined that I didn't want to be cleaning pools forever, my mother and I made the trip up to the great lakes and to watch my brother graduate from Navy boot camp. I'll never forget the admiration and the overwhelming pride that my family felt towards my brother, and he moved with a swagger that he never had prior to leaving for boot camp.

After we visited him, my mother and grandmother went out to get some food and celebrate a little while I stayed back in to hotel room. I used that time alone to scroll through the Internet and research different branches of the military, I knew that if I was going to join that I would have to one up my brother, so I had to decide between the Army or the Marine Corps. It did not take long for me to figure out that the Marines were definitely known for their reputation of being hardcore and the best branch to join, go big or go home, am I right? I decided to take a bath and contemplate my decisions. Staring at the ceiling think about my future I had finally decided that if I was going to join the military than it absolutely had to be the Marines. If only I knew what the future had in store for me in that moment.

Upon returning home from my brother's graduation in Chicago, my mind was already made up, I just wasn't sure what I had to do next. It wasn't hard to figure out that recruiters make it very easy to get in contact with them. I was at a gas station before work and I saw and ad board where people like to pin up their business cards, ads to sell vehicles, or looking for a lost pet. This was like the original craigslist. Below the little board there was a stack of neatly placed business cards on the shelf, which stuck out compared to the messy piles placed next to it. My young naïve mind thought, 'oh this must be a sign,' so I grabbed a business card and got back into my truck. I was headed to a pool-cleaning job about 45 minutes away, so I decided to say fuck it and call this recruiter. I dialed the number and on the second ring a voice answered;

"Good afternoon Sgt Cruise, United States Marines how can I help you?" His smooth and confident voice boomed over the line, giving me

Goosebumps and making me feel even more nervous than I had been before.

"Uh yeah hi, um I was thinking about joining the Marines, us sir," I responded shakily. I'm not going to spell out the whole conversation that I had with him because that would just ruin the whole speech that recruiters give you to reel you in, but let's just say from the moment he started talking I was hooked on every word.

    The thing that impressed me the most was how fast he wanted me to come in. I was on my way home that same day, coming from my last pool job and he wanted me to stop by the office. Little did I know at that time I was probably the Miracle call he got to go home that day, but regardless I was impressed with how available he was. You don't wear business casual clothing when you clean pools; it's usually a tank top, basketball shorts, and flip-flops. Sgt Cruise pretty much said it was cool that I came in looking like a bum even though I felt uncomfortable showing up to his office looking like a sweaty and disgusting mess from being out in the hot sun all day.

I sat in the parking lot just staring at the office door while my heart was pounding a millions times per minute. They tell you that the yellow foot prints is the moment your life will change forever, well I call bullshit because the moment that I walked into that recruiter's office, my life changed in so many ways. Regardless of how you came into the military, at one point in your life you had to walk into a recruiter's office and decide what you wanted to do about your future.

It took me mustering up all of the testosterone in my balls to get out of the car and walk towards the door that day. I walked into the office and I shit you not, this man looked like Tom Cruise on steroids. I reached my hard towards his outstretched one and it was the firmest handshake that I had ever received. This guy goes through every speech in the book to reel me in and takes down all of my information. I found out that since I was attending Palmetto Ridge High that Sgt Dung would be my recruiter. At the time I didn't think much about it but for every good recruiter there is a shitty one who makes people turn away from actually joining the military, and let's just say that Sgt Dung was not one of the good recruiters.

    I went home after my meeting with this guy and wondered how my parents were going to take the news, I was really nervous, so I decided to procrastinate the whole thing. I wasn't 18 quite yet so I knew that I was going to have to have my parents sign some of the paperwork, and I knew it had to be soon. Sgt Dung scheduled a time for me to bring my parents in to talk to them and fill out some paperwork. Before going I sat down with them and explained to them what my decision was. My mom instantly started crying and my dad was trying to convince me that maybe I should look into a different branch. At this point, my mind was already made up so I told them that the Marines was my choice and that was it. I took them to my recruiting office and Sgt Dung showed them multiple motivational videos, which got me even more hyped up and started to ease my parent's minds. I had an easy contract with one a waiver for smoking weed.

The next thing he did was pull out the benefit tags, they're like thick business cards that say different things that the Marine Corps can offer you, such as travel, fitness and education. For me, my recruiter had me pick three of them and he explained what kind of possibilities I had in the Marines to be able to do the things that I wanted to do. People assume that their recruiter will remember everything that they like but in reality they don't really give a fuck, so they just plug your answers into a little spread sheet that they can come back to later when they need it.

Talking about jobs was the part I was most excited about, my obvious first choice was infantry, which made my parents start to freak out and beg me not to choose it because they thought I would die. It isn't as easy to get into the infantry as people may think because the spots fill up super-fast. I wasn't fully into going infantry just because I've heard awful stories about how bad it could be and I wasn't a huge fan of long hikes. I thought driving tanks would be cool as hell so that's what I told Sgt Dung I wanted to do, I wanted to have a badass job.

    This was where I should have realized that Sgt Dung was kind of a piece of shit. I told him that I wanted to be a tank operator and he came back with a contract that said CD and had 5 different jobs listed, none with the word tank in the title. He started talking about how heavy equipment and tanks go hand in hand, and promised that I would get plenty of time riding in tanks. To this day, in all 8 years that I have been in the Marine Corps, I have not been in a tank or watched one in action. I was a teenager at the time and I didn't have the balls to call Sgt Dung out on his bullshit, so the next 4 years of my life were drastically different than what I was expecting.

What made it really obvious that Sgt Dung only cared about his numbers and not about the people he was recruiting is that he sent me to the Military Entrance Processing Station (MEPS) the day after my birthday. The night of my 18th birthday was spent alone in a hotel room 3 hours away from my friends and family. He didn't even offer to buy my food on the trip out there. I found out years after this happened that recruiters are allocated money to buy poolees (people who are in the DEP waiting to go to boot camp) food while they are going through MEPS, this upset me because at the time I only had like $20 to my name and I had to make it last for two days while I was stuck in a hotel.

MEPS is the first little taste of the military that anyone gets, I spent damn near 12 hours in this windowless hospital type building going through a bunch of steps with 20 random strangers, doing things from getting my blood drawn, pissing in a cup, and getting my nuts checked out by some 80 year old doctor. Long story short it's really a long boring day with no cellphones, shitty food, and just over all terrible time. Thankfully I managed not to say anything dumb through the process and this allowed me to be able to sign my contract and swear into the Delayed Entry Program (DEP) since I was still in high school. Some guys who are there for the final time get to sign their contracts and immediately ship off to either Parris Island, SC or San Diego, CA. The DEP is the first step on the official pathway to becoming a Marine, while at MEPS they give you the date you'll leave for boot camp, a bunch of Marine swag, and put you in a loop with other poolees in your area.

  In Marine Corps, one thing they take pride in is physical fitness, and with that we do way more running than is probably necessary. One thing that I really did not like back then and to this day still can't stand, is running. I have tried time and time again to start running and enjoy it but it's just not something that I can get into. I will say though, I'm way better at running now than I was when I first joined, but regardless my opinion of it hasn't really changed over the years.

Being a poolee, we did these things called an Initial Strength Test (IST), which consists of a max set of pull-ups, at least 100 crunches in 2 minutes, and a mile and a half run. The pull ups and the crunches didn't really bother me at all, I couldn't do all 20 pull ups but being a weak 18 year old who didn't really work out I could knock out anywhere from 15-18 depending on the day, and I could knock out all the crunches pretty easy. As for the running, the maximum passing run time was 13 minutes or less for males and for me, meeting the time was a serious struggle.

Sgt Dung, being the world-class recruiter that he was had one of the poolees who was fast at running coach me. This poolee was 6'4 and maybe 150 pounds soaking wet, his running capabilities were all genetics and that was pointless for me because I needed someone who had more of techniques and exercises that would help me improve my running. This was the start of me discovering that just because you're in the military, doesn't mean you can't be a piece of shit too.

One day during a PT session, the recruiters needed to run their Physical Fitness Test (PFT) and instead of doing two separate work outs, they just had us complete it with them. We started out with the crunches and I was next to Sgt Dung, he wasn't moving as fast as I was and when the guy keeping track of times yells that we have 10 seconds left, I had to speed up to knock out the last few, I barely made it with 2 seconds to spare. When the score keeper went around for scores, Sgt Dung told him that he did all 100, but there was no way in hell that he did if I barely made it to 100 myself.

Armed with some new knowledge on how easy it is to lie on PT scores I started to see that the only thing that keeps the scores honest is a person's integrity. You may be wondering how, well when you are completing an exercise, like the pull ups or crunches, there is someone counting out your reps, and someone score keeping, these are usually two different people and the score keeper doesn't keep track of your score for you, they just write down what you tell them. So you may do 12 pull ups but when you walk over to the score keeper you can easily tell them that you did 18. While the crunches are the easiest to cheat, if you're paired up with a friend they'll usually skip numbers discreetly so you get the full score, but the run is the hardest to cheat because most courses are a down and back course. But this time when we ran it, it was 5 laps around the park and most people would only complete 4 and lie to say that they did 5. Even if you run the full 5, sometimes the scorekeeper isn't within earshot and you can shave a minute or two off your time without them noticing. Granted I didn't fully learn how a lot of that stuff worked until I was in for a while, but I got my first taste of it while in the DEP.

Being in the DEP felt like I was in limbo, most people will tell you that it's a time where your recruiter will guide you and give you tips to help you be successful at boot camp, telling you stories, and giving you as much wisdom as they can. But not Sgt Dung, he decided that he would lose all the paperwork I'd turn in, more than once, then when I got to MEPS I'd be missing something, so I'd have to go back again. I'm pretty sure to this day that I hold the record for the most trips to MEPS by a single poolee in my area with no health issues. I made 10 trips to MEPS within the 8 months that I was in the DEP. The 3 hour road trips each way, more than once a month really started to frustrate me and when I brought it up to Sgt Dung he would say;

"Well if you want to be a Marine, then this is the shit you have to do, good to go?" I asked around and every other poolee around me was confused because they went once, maybe twice at the most if they needed a waiver.

I didn't really start to hate Sgt Dung until my 10th and final time going through MEPS prior to leaving for boot camp. Sgt Dung dropped me off at some shady gas station on the other side of town around sunset and I was told that another recruiter was going to come and get me. I sat at this gas station for close to three hours when a homeless looking dude started walking my way. He asked me if I had any spare change, and when I said no this mad leaped towards me and grabbed me to try to reach into my pockets. I was scared as hell but I managed to shove him as hard as I could and he flew back what seemed like 10 feet. He wasn't really big or strong and I could have beaten the crap out of him, but being a white boy from the suburbs I had never really been in a fight with anyone other than white boys from the suburbs, so I ran inside. The guy working in the gas station saw what happened and informed me that he had already called the police.

Luckily for me I made the right choice by running inside because when the cops searched the man's pockets he had a pocketknife on him. The police took my statement and made sure I was okay before taking the man back to the station. Forgetting about my ride in the moment I realized it was almost 9 pm and I still hadn't been picked up yet. I called the recruiter of the century and sure enough when he picked up, he was hammered, "Heya Sgt Dung USSSS Marines How can I help ya?"

"So when is my ride getting here? It's been over 3 hours." I responded and he fucking hung up on me. I was extremely pissed off at this point, ready to just say fuck it and not even go to boot camp, I could just stay and clean pools.

Before saying fuck it to everything, I tried one more thing. The Marine in charge of the Entire Recruiting station is called a Staff Non-commissioned Officer in Charge (SNCOIC). Gunnery Sergeant Vanderbilt was the SNCOIC, he wasn't the greatest Marine, but he took pride in his work and was pretty respectable. I decided to give him a call before calling my parents, I explained everything that happened within the last few hours and within 15 minutes I had a recruiter there ready to take me to MEPS. Looking back at that day GYSGT Vanderbilt saved Sgt Dung's ass from getting in trouble, but at the time I just thought he was looking out for me.

After finishing at MEPS the next day, Sgt Dung called me, hung over as fuck and started screaming at me over the phone about how some kid thinks he can just jump over his head and tell his boss about my situation, and that he was going to get me a "dishonorable discharge" from the Marines (I know that a lie, but I didn't know that when I was 18.), he told me I was a complete bitch and I wouldn't last if I couldn't figure it out for myself. Being an 18 year old with no hair on my balls, I took it without saying a word.

Months went by and I thought Sgt Dung was

trying to make amends with me and possibly felt bad for what happened that night, but this was where I learned about "office politics". This dude was always acting nice around me, but the moment I left he would bad mouth my name like it was his job. That's beside the point though, I was back on board and motivated about the Marines again. While in the DEP there is a way to get promoted from E-1 to E-2 if you get 2 people to enlist as well. While it may only be a few hundred dollars extra a month, it sets you months ahead of your peers in the eyes of a promotion and that's what I was really striving towards. Being as motivated as I was at the time, I went out to try and recruit some of my loser high school friends, but most of them just laughed at me. However, when graduation go closer reality really started to kick in for most of them and I managed to get three guys to come and talk to Sgt Dung. All three of them specifically told Sgt Dung that I referred them and all three of them ended up enlisting successfully, did their time, and one is even a drill instructor right now. But Sgt Dung being the weasel he was decided that I didn't rate the promotion so I never go it and sure enough I started as an E-1 Private at the beginning of my career.

In the month of July 2012 I had started to get all of my paperwork double checked by the station to make sure I was go to go so I would be able to leave at the end of the month. They checked everything, waivers, weight, and physical fitness before sending you off to boot camp. Heading off to Miami with over 200 poolees from around the state that were shipping off between July and August. We went there to get our fitness test, weigh in's done, and the Sergeant Major showed up to oversee everything. When doing the height and weight I passed with flying colors. Next came the IST, something I despised more than I did Sgt Dung. I got through the pull-ups and crunches without any issues, but starting the race I started out way too fast and at that time I didn't know how bad a fast start could affect an overall finish. About three quarters of a mile through I start getting passed a lot and went from the running speed of a gazelle, to the speed of an aggressive snail. I was completely gassed out and struggling miserably. When I saw the finish line I mustered up all the energy in my body and raced through the finish line and heard a time of 13:10. I remember heading straight for a trashcan and vomiting before heading to the cool down circle. The passing time to leave for boot camp was 13:00 and I failed by 10 seconds. When they started asking everyone what their run times were, I got nervous, but when my name was called I stuttered out a quick "uh thirteen".

The guy laughed before responding with, "damn man you barley made it."

    I felt like a piece of shit for lying, I didn't want to begin my career on a lie, but I also didn't want my ship date to get pushed back. At that time I still believed in the idea of honor, courage, commitment and I had made a bed of lies to lay in.

    The day came where it was finally time to head down to MEPS and officially leave for boot camp. I had my final weekend of partying with friends and spending time with my family before leaving. I decided to wear a nice flannel shirt and very tight jeans with my favorite pair of Jordan's, which were all a big mistake that I later learned (I'll come back to this later). My parents dropped me off at the recruiting station the day before my father's birthday, and it had been the first time I ever witnessed him cry. They weren't getting out of the car with me so I hugged them both before I got out and walked into the office without looking back.

    The night in the hotel was really uncomfortable, I had left my phone with my parents and the only things that I brought with me were a folder with all of my paperwork and a travel size toothbrush and toothpaste my parents had bought for me that morning, which I just ended up leaving at the hotel anyway. I walked over to the liquor store across the street and bought myself a pack of cigarettes even though I didn't smoke, but I figured it was something people did before going to boot camp. I was right, three other guys were there doing the same thing, all being different branches, we didn't really talk to each other, just stood around awkwardly.

The morning came and I didn't sleep for shit, but I still felt really energetic because this was something that I had been waiting for. I had watched every video I could find on the Internet about boot camp and I thought I was ready for anything, I swore I knew how it all was going to be. I thought I was ready, boy was I wrong.

Going to MEPS to get our final paperwork, plane tickets, and the $20 check for food, we were put on a bus to the airport. I grouped up with a few other guys because one of them knew how to navigate through an airport and two of them ended up being in my boot camp platoon. We stuck out with our huge folders of paperwork the entire time and the Marines who were waiting for us to arrive at the airport spotted us from a mile away. They loaded a bunch of us onto a bus and told us to put our heads down as they took us on the longest ride to the gate of Parris Island, SC, our new home for the next three months.

I had been preparing to be bossed around for months and I complied with everything. Some people were stupid enough to lift their head, making the Marine who got us from the airport in the front scream at them to put their heads down. Once we finally arrived at the yellow footprints, that guy with the funny hat walked on and gave the same speech you see in all the videos on the internet.

Chapter 2- Bootcamp

Marine Corps Recruit Depot, Parris Island, South Carolina if you know anything about the Marine Corps then you probably have heard of this place. It's a love but mostly hate place with here. When arriving here you spend what feels like about 3 days awake in the same clothes you have worn since you left your recruiter office. Every one tells you to wear proper civilian attire which is correct. If you don't wear nice clothes you're going to get that ass reamed by the guys with the funny hats on. But my two cents of advice don't forget to wear something comfortable and can run around in for about three days.

    I felt so dirty wearing those clothes for soo long. Another topic no one mentions is showering isn't really much of a thing either till you get all of the receiving paperwork and initial check in task complete. Soo just imagine this you have the same clothes on after running around getting screamed at, you just got all your hair shaved off with what feels like a rusty butter knife, and last time you showered was the morning you left the hotel. It's a pretty musky scent you have after it's all done and over.

While in the middle of all this chaos you hardly will remember because you're tired and in a complete different environment you get these big green bags with a bunch of uniforms that are either way too small or too tight and hygiene items. While carrying this around you and about 80 guys your about to become real close with go up to one of these squad bays above where all of this bull shit has been going on. It was here for the first time I have ever got naked with about 80 other men all at once.

Now I played some sports in high school been in plenty of locker rooms being around naked guys wasn't that new to me. But this is not the same in high school you have towels, you're not in a rush for the most part, and you don't have these angry guys with funny hats running around screaming at you. Putting on tighty whities in that situation was unique to say the least. But let me tell you the relief we all had when finally taking off our sweaty nasty civilian clothes was the best feeling in that portion of recruit training.

One part they never get mentioned is the medical aspect. When you have hundreds of people all doing the same thing the only way to do it is by the numbers. Going through medical process the herd you in line like farm animals and people with closed fist stab you with all of these shots. But the worst of the shots is without a doubt the peanut butter shot. They have you in line drop your pants and expose your ass and shoot you with a needle that is about as thick as a pen with penicillin. But its not like they get it perfect so how do you get the penicillin in the blood stream you might ask? You and all of your new best friends sit down and roll back and forth on your ass getting it nice and rubbed in properly. No matter how you image it the result is just ridiculous 80 plus men all sitting down rolling around on there ass just not what you think of when the most elite warriors on the planet comes to mind. But everyone that isn't allergic to the shot does it.

As the days go by we get sorted up into our platoons and the drill instructors (guys with the funny hats, google it) who deal with our initial receiving stuff take us to our squad bay. In the movies they usually show the old buildings made of concrete and just have that old military vibe, atleast that was what I was expecting due to how the receiving building had that similar feel. We get outside and start walking toward the buildings and Im just hoping I'm on the first floor because being on the third floor just sounds like a recipe for a bad time. We keep walking and we past the building where all the other platoons are going. Im started to get slightly confused until I saw my new home for three months.

Right next to the building where everyone else went was this monster size double wide trailer. Not going to lie it took me a second to comprehend it. Sure enough we all pile up in there with our big heavy bags of stuff and start getting set up for our new life. The next few days was odd we fount out the drill instructors that have been walking us around weren't going to be with us for the duration. It was kind of a relief one of them had some pretty serious issues. When we were taking our turn showering for the first time since getting there one of my fellow recruits said out aloud "man this feels so good". I shit you not this man in his full uniform walked right into the shower right next to this naked man cover in soap and said "You think that feels good wait till the lights go off I'll give you something that will feel real good". At this time the don't ask don't tell policy was just lifted so it wasn't a punishable offence I suppose but I definitely wasn't upset I wouldn't be with that guy for 3 months.

After that awkward interaction we started to get the last few things needed before we started our "official" recruit training which was the rifle and CIF gear (honestly don't know what cif stands for but its all the field gear we have like packs, rifle magazine cases, canteens, and etc). Just like everything else so far it was a hurry up and wait around process. But at the end of the day Thursday we had all of our gear and were ready to take off our running shoes and put on boots which means we are officially "recruits training".

Black Friday if you ever seen a YouTube video about boot camp that was probably it. One thing the Marine Corps does is having the same structure over a period of time. For the most part my black Friday experience was most likely the same as everyone elses down to the speech the drill instructors give the same as everyone else's within the last 10-15 years or probably even more. We are really good believers of the saying if it isn't broke don't fix it method.

    For my platoon 2083 I had four drill instructors and they all had different responsibilities. The first is the Senior Drill instructor. As the name states he is the senior and in charge of the other drill instructors and generally the most level head that keeps the others in check. This Man's name was Staff sergeant McDonald he was a really fit guy about 6 foot 3 and had a really athletic build. The next was called the Heavy he was the second in charge and was responsible for teaching us how to march and dealing with any our gear issues. This Marines name was Sgt Mount he was in pretty good shape not as athletic as McDonald's. But you could tell he could keep up with anyone. Kind of looked like a who from who Ville in the Grinch. The second two there jobs were solely to just fuck us up on a daily and just make life a living hell they were the newer drill instructors and their names was SSgt Horsley and SSgt Roberts, they weren't in the best shape but still a better runner then me. Horsley at the time we all hated him more than anyone because of the role he was in but afterwards he was actually a genuinely good person and Roberts honestly was the funniest one of the bunch without even noticing it.

Black Friday kicks off and just like the videos you have probably seen we are all getting tore up running around dumping stuff picking stuff up the whole nine yards.

There's no point in really going into that because it's out on the Internet. Let me tell you about the aftermath. Eventually they have to stop fucking you up because there is a schedule believe it or not every day. There is a lot of structure your days are pre planned out down to the hour for the most part. So once make the recruits run around and get all sweaty time is over, we have things to do like going to classes or going have lunch. One way to compare it is like being in a house with abusive parents. Imagine just being home getting your ass kicked then picking everything up, cleaning yourself up, and going out in public and acting like you're okay. That is literally the daily routine, some days you don't get messed up some days you're in the middle of the trailer holding a rifle with your arms locked out for 10-15 minutes. It's quite the abusive relationship between you and the drill instructors.

A lot of people think boot camp is just a lot of physical training, funny thing is you do more physical training after boot camp then while you're there. Would you like to know how many times we did actual no shit running in like the little green shorts for more than half a mile? Literally no less than 10 times. It's kind of ironic and no one thinks much about it but when you think about it but the drill instructors spend most of your time there teaching you how to wait for it…Drill. Drill is the how we do all our marching tricks with the turns and movements as one big group. Out of my time there I marched more miles then I ran by a significant amount.

It takes awhile but eventually you start to get into the routine of recruit training. You accept you have no sense of time, you wake up at stupid early, you do literally everything by the numbers down to putting socks on, and it's kind of like being a prisoner. But you learn to adapt and not cause unnecessary attention to yourself and just try and keep that up for three months.

One thing that to this day still confuses me though. One day Sgt Mount woke us up and was pissed as hell don't know why, but he said "there's a hurricane coming " I somehow knew he wasn't talking about the weather mostly because it was clear sky and just didn't seem that bad of weather. So he keeps rambling about that as we are on our way to breakfast. Usually we got about 20-30 minutes to eat sometimes more sometimes less. That day I sat down for about 45 seconds and was told to get up and go outside by Sgt Mount. I crammed as much food in my mouth on my way to throwing my tray out as possible, I had a feeling this man was about to do something that wouldn't be fun. We start marching back and he is the only drill instructor there. Usually by this time all of them are there ready for the day. We head inside and we learnt what he meant by hurricane. This man had us empty every personal item we had in to the middle of our trailer aka squad bay. I stuffed my letters and wallet inside my pants at the time that was the only thing important too me. He has us slide all of our shoes, beds, backpacks, foot lockers, into the center of the squad bay. After that we figured nothing else he could possibly do. Boy was we wrong we pushed everything and I mean everything into the shower room. The shower room was only about the size of a 1 car garage. We had about 80 beds, lockers, shoes, and personal items. Lets just say it was a tight squeeze. We got it all in there somehow and sure enough the water had to come on. After that we spent the next couple hours cleaning everything up obviously. But the one part that still gets me to this day. Everyone and I mean everyone got all of there stuff back we worked well as a team ensuring every letter, every sock, everything we owned was returned to its proper owner.

Theres was one exception, I somehow ended up with a size 7 right foot running shoe and a size 11 left foot running shoe. I went to every single person in that platoon for days and asked if they had two different size running shoes. I even said I would take the size they didn't want to all 80 plus people in my platoon. Not one single person offered to trade. There was someone there who had two different size shoes and had to be ok with it and out of all the things that happened there it still does not make sense to me. I went to everyone personally through out the training cycle and would have been no effort on their part at all. But one of those guys wanted two different size shoes.

Being a recruit and being a prisoner have a lot in common. After you've been there for a few months you start to try and see what you can get away with. Toward the later part of the training you do a thing called field week. It's basically like a lower tempo week to kind of give the recruits and drill instructors a break before the high tempo training that concludes the training cycle. A few recruits go get their teeth taken care and the rest go do work details to maintain the base. These work details include things such as doing laundry for everyone, mowing grass, cleaning buildings, and just overall cleaning. Soo as ironic as it could be one of these days I got sent to clean the pool where we do our swim training. How shitty is that I joined the Marines to not clean pools and what do they have me doing? Cleaning one of the only pools on that damn base. Doing that work detail is the first time I tried chewing tobacco. Being in recruit training you have a very good diet. All you drink is water maybe sneak the powerade in every now and again.

For food you have a meat for protein like chicken or fish, a clean carb like rice or maybe a potato, a vegetable, and maybe a cookie if you're lucky. That's why everyone loses the weight at boot camp and just being on your feet a lot. But beside the point your body has no tolerance to any bad substance like tobacco. We are leaving the pool and as I grab the trash I notice a can of grizzly wintergreen I figure its empty but when I grab it and shake it's was literally a brand new can unopened. I didn't really think much of it but one of my boys said it was awesome so we all take turns putting a dip in. We made sure to make them nice and compact so on our way marching back to the trailer no one would notice it. When we started walking back I experienced a buzz like I have never had before. My head had this high I have never experienced to this day. My body had this amazingly numb feeling that I never wanted to go away.

When we get back we all made sure to spit the dip out and hid them underneath the trailer we called the squad bay. We rinsed our mouths out and walked in still on the nicotine high. During our time at the pool someone got caught sneaking peanut butter packets back into the squad bay which was basically a death wish for a recruit. So as we were holding our rifles out in front of us my nicotine high wore off really quick. To this day I still dislike that peanut butter stealing bitch for killing my buzz.

While you get along with almost everyone in your platoon there's just bound to be one or two people you just don't mesh with. For me it was this guy named Gooch. In a nutshell this dude worshipped the devil, screwed everyone over, was awkward, and just flat out a douche bag. I just so happened to share bunk beds with him. In the mornings if we was good they would let us make our own beds and get ready at our own pace. Every other group all worked together made there beds then got dressed. Your boy gooch decided he didn't feel like making his bed and just wanted to get dressed and let someone else do it for him. Working as a team is the main point of boot camp but being selfish like that just isn't the way. I call him out on this several times and he just ran away. I let this boil up for about 3 weeks. One night when we are all getting ready to go to sleep we all have our little bed side conversations once the drill instructor goes away. I was talking to the guy next to me and said something along the lines "It would be nice to not have to make Gooch's bed every morning". This little bitch replies in a nazzley high pitched tone "why don't you make me do it bitch". I jump off my top rack look this pathetic man in the eyes and he covers his face with the blanket. I lose my shit and decide he doesn't deserve a bed since he won't make it. I pull this boy out of his bed into the middle of the squad bay. Just as I'm about to hit him with the uppercut I see the lights come on.

Ssgt McDonald appears outside the office where the drill instructors sleep and do their paperwork in. I shit you not from there office to my bed was about 35-40 feet away and he didn't run he teleported right to me and wrapped my arm back before I could even pull it back to hit gooch.

    As much as drill instructors are mean and dicks all the time he gave me some legit man advice. He said "check it out beach, I know gooch is a bitch I want to choke slam that bitch on a daily. But guess what happens if he has a black eye? Your ass is getting dropped and staying here for way longer then you want possibly getting charged with assault". From that day I always had a special respect for Ssgt McDonald.
What happened to gooch you may ask? Well I got him back in another way. Definitely way more sadistic and well if you got this far this is where it starts to get a lot dirtier and probably funnier part of the story. Every night

before we go to sleep we set out all of our clothes and stuff we need for the next day.

By the time we get to the rifle range we are at about 5 to 6 weeks into recruit training. The rifle range wasn't close to where my trailer squad bay home was so we moved closer for the two weeks while we was at the rifle range into more classic squad bays. The perks of this is they have these things called pillars where you kind of hide behind. At night we always have a couple recruits up making sure nothing crazy happens like punching gooch in the face. This night super late or early whatever you want to call it I decide it is time to get my revenge on gooch. I grab his socks, boots, canteen and head into the "Head" aka bathroom using the pillars as cover so the fire watch didn't see me. I decided it was time to relieve myself. I piss over everything of his. Not the most prideful moment of my life but damn did it feel good?

Now I have gotten my revenge on gooch and feel fine. But let it be known there was quite a bit of people who hated him beside me. About 78 other gooch haters to be exact. I don't know the details of it all but back then our rifles had iron sights and the way you get them aligned is by adjusting a small screw with a flat head or just anything made of metal honestly. Someone the night before rifle qualification went to his rifle and messed up his sights. The day we had to qualify he failed. What they do when you fail is during that week of down time we got to clean the base your given you a chance to qualify again. But he failed every time that week and was dropped from our platoon. I would have almost felt bad for anyone else but to be honest the little cock sucker had it coming.

When you move in with 80 people from all around the country into a fairly small place and do everything together, getting sick is inevitable. Everyone gets sick at one point or another from the common cold to pneumonia sometimes-even tuberculosis. Late into the cycle a couple days before we start the crucible (the culminating event for recruit training) this guy name Hook got real sick. I really respected Hook he was a little bit older than most of us about 23. But just all around a really good guy couldn't march worth a dam but just a real team player the drill instructors hated his lack of drill skill but even they knew he was going to be a great Marine. Two day before the crucible he starts coughing up blood and this guy has been a trooper the whole time getting messed up worse then everyone almost daily we all really respected him. Finally the day before he taps out and goes to get checked by a doctor. He comes back with a mask on reveals to everyone he got Tuberculosis and was getting dropped. I never felt so bad for anyone in my life. I didn't know much about TB but I knew it took awhile to treat. He grabbed all his things and that was the last time we saw him. Even the drill instructors came out after he left and gave him some kudos which is not something they are known for doing. It really killed the attitude of the platoon going in to the crucible.

On a good note though several months after boot camp I hit him up and discovered he managed to get cured of TB in about 3 months went back to a training platoon and graduated the top Marine in his company.

The week leading up to officially graduating feels like an entirety. You're officially Marines so the drill instructors aren't really messing with you anymore but you're still a boot. Getting plane tickets to go the next step is a bit of a process. Imagine a hand full of administrative guys having to buy plane tickets for over 200 plus Marines. It takes a bit of time. But the day comes eventually and you march across the parade deck. What's funny is while most Parents want to talk to the drill instructors and thank them for changing the child and see the whole place. I can speak honestly on the behalf of most drill instructors and boot camp graduate's. We all just want to go home get drunk, have sex, and sleep in. But we stay and take the pictures for our families.

Chapter 3-Boot leave and MCT

If I had to imagine what it's like leaving a concentration camp I would compare it to leaving Parris Island. As you leave Parris island its really weird at first. I didn't know if I was supposed to act like the boot they just molded me in to keep selling the Marines or if I could be myself. It took me a couple days before I finally started act myself again but even then I still did all the typical boot things. For my luck all of those social media pages weren't a thing so I missed out being on that, lord knows I should have been. When you go home for those 10 days it's suppose to show the world pretty much hey look what the Marines did to that loser they could fix anyone.

When your home it's a really confusing time you want to show off but you also want relax a bit. I spent my first night putting my dress blues together; I was up till like 11pm just to take a retarded picture in it. Then your parents are going to want to go and show you off to everyone which is kind of fun. But the main thing I wanted to try out was the seeing if those blues really got you laid trick. For me after about day 7 of boot leave you start realize you can be a person again and its time to party.

My first experience of getting laid as a Marine is quite the tale. Like I said I wasn't the most popular kid in high school to where they would throw a huge party for me coming home from boot camp. But there happened to be a house party toward the end of my boot leave and it all kind of worked out to where I could see a bunch of my "friends". Fast forward I'm at this party we are all having a good time. My friend Blake basically has the connect with all the hoes at this party. I just got out of the pool and went in the shower. Blake asks me "yo Dathan trying to get laid right now?" Me haven't had sex now in a bit over 3 months reply "FUCK YES!! WHO??" he said, "Vanessa is in the other bedroom and she wants to smash". I finished my shower at recruit speed and am out the bathroom and into the bedroom in about 10 seconds. I try to play it all cool and have a little bit of foreplay but I'm hammered as hell.

    I go in trying to use my new Marine vocabulary she took off her shirt and I said "oh very well shirts are off the body". I wish I could have punched myself in the dick for saying that, I deserved it. We start making out I had way more confidence then I really should. I start doing the ol finger blasting technique. I do that for a little bit. Then she decides it time to smash. We both drop our pants. I thank god didn't try and say trousers off the body. I bend her over doggy style and as much as it hurts my pride to say this I came before I even got it in. Three months of no ejaculating really does a number on you. I try and play it off put on another condom but it just didn't work. She kind of smiles and bless her heart just leaves going into another room. I sit there a lot more sober then I was about 15 seconds earlier and decided I needed to turn up again get my drunk on. I waited about 15 minutes so it didn't seem like I was a complete premature ejaculator then came out everyone gave me dabs and the night went on till I blacked out. Vanessa was the real MVP for keeping that on the Down low for me though.

The 10 days of leave post boot camp go by super quick. You almost forget you still have another 3 years and 9 months left on your contract. On your final days you start to pack all of your bags and make sure you have everything you need for the next step which is Marine combat training also known as MCT. One thing I can attribute to the military is you learn how to navigate airports really quick. You go through airports about 5 plus times in your first year, most of my friends back home have never even been on a plane before.

Marine combat training is a month long of teaching you how to be a "grunt". On Paper it sounds like a good time you shoot Machine guns, grenade launchers, throw hand grenades, and learn how to clear houses. Sounds good in theory but there's always more to it than just what's on paper. By the time you get to MCT it is a weird place you think your ready to be treated like "real Marines" and be responsible enough to handle yourself but in all reality your still just as helpless as you was about three months prior when you arrived to Parris Island the only thing is now your more cocky.

Checking in for MCT is the first time you ever see your typical day to day Marine. These are the guys just trying to have a good time and get the job done. There usually not much older then you and been in like a year or so. They have some papers for you; show you where you're going to be sleeping for the night, and get you ready for the morning. The best part about checking into MCT is seeing all the guys you went to boot camp with its nice seeing familiar faces.

    MCT is not even half as bad as boot camp. I got to wear clean uniforms I wasn't running around aimlessly and the person in charge of us wasn't creepy as hell quite the improvement from last time. It still has its annoying factors just like anything that involves with dealing with 100s of Marines all at the same time. We walked around did our drug test, got our paper work turned in, get medically checked out, and it only took us one normal day to get it all done. The next part though was the biggest shocker for me.

When we get ready to move our stuff out to our permeant squad bay for the remainder of the training we was lined up next to female Marines. Now I did in fact knew they existed even saw a few from far at boot camp but we was always kept pretty far from them and if they were anywhere near us they were there just to talk to the drill instructors. Probably because they were all smashing one another. But back to the point I was literally standing right next to one for the first time and I was pretty confused. But that confusion slowly went away and learnt some things about female Marines that I'll get too later.

Your Combat instructors are not nearly as influential as your drill instructors. They know that and its okay everyone accepts the next month is just an enormous waste of government spending, but might as well make the best of it. . I had three instructors I remember anyway Sergeant Sikes who was a actual grunt that somehow got stuck training all of us non grunts he was very discontent about it. I remember he had a bit of a case of napoleon disorder he wasn't a very tall man and when we did hikes he really had to flex on everyone, to the point where he would strap weights on his pack. Then we had Ssgt Vohn I swear this man had to be at least 50 years old I later fount out he was only 31 but the Marines ages some people harder then others. He reminded me of mermaid man from SpongeBob. Then last was Ssgt Daniels she was one of those mom figures, she tried to take care of us but sometimes we honestly just needed a real ass whopping. After we meet all of them we do our cell phone turn. Some people didn't do it, me at the time I was a little bitch and did but if I could go back I definitely would have kept it could have been the ultimate bargain chip.

MCT is where Marines learn about the field life. One aspect to the field life is we trade like a damn swap meet. You got cheese spread ill trade you for chocolate. You got skittles I got M&Ms that's just the PG trades they everyone sees. Then there is the behind the scenes trades. Remember how I told you there was people who didn't turn in their phone. Well we had guys selling phone calls for like 40 to 50 bucks. Everyone brings cash out there because they have a little store where you can buy "necessities" like socks and razors. This is where the true hustlers of the Marine Corps start to emerge. Obviously we aren't supposed to have tobacco products but the guys trying to make quick bucks out there are selling cigarettes for 5 bucks a smoke. The best part is the instructors try to keep us from doing it but out meals literally have matches in them. But that isn't even the worse part there was one thing all of us 18-20 year old guys wanted and it for the first time was right next door, the women.

There's really no proper way to put this but I have gotten my dick sucked for a bag of skittles by a female Marine because of MCT. The ultimate bargain tool throughout that course was female companionship. It's not as glorious as you probably think. When it happens it's usually super late in the night at the time it was winter so imagine about 20-degree weather usually inside a porta-potty. The second major problem was due to it being cold no one showered and after about three weeks everyone started to really smell. If you're reading this I'm going to assume you want the story behind skittles. When I was in line next to the first female Marine I ever encountered I immediately sparked up a conversation. We talked about where we both were from what we use to do making small talk. Her name was Erin; over the next few days we would say hi to each other in passing and wouldn't necessarily go out of our way to be in line with each other but didn't quite avoid it either. As the time goes by we make our way out to the field were we do all the cool stuff that was on paper. Our unit was getting ready to conduct the night shooting. Its kind of a joke no one really aims its just more or less a complete waste of money me and Erin just so happened to be shooting next to me as we finish shooting and make our way off the firing line she mentions how hungry she is and is pissed they aren't giving us any more MRE's (meal ready to eat aka shitty brown bags of food they give us in the field) I inform her I have some skittles back in our sleeping area.

    Our sleeping areas for men and women are separated by a big piece of plywood. She said "I will do anything for them". Naïve and me being young tell her "Just when you we get back to our sleeping area just knock on the wall and I'll met you by the port-potty's". She said okay and I didn't think much about it. We finish up getting all our rifles cleared make sure everything is good and get ready for bed. My rack was right next to the "divider" I'm laying down and here the three knocks. I remembered our deal and totally forgot about it. I whisper, "I'm on my way give me 5 minutes". I get dressed real quick grab the skittles and head out the door. We meet up and she had a different look to her. I go to hand her the skittles and she looks at me smiling says "you get anything you want" at this point I'm young and dumb but not that dumb so I grab her and head straight for the instructor port-potty's. Why would I pick the instructor one you might ask? Well when 300 plus Marines are pooping and peeing in the same 10 port-potty's it really kills the mood with the stench. Where we are at is pretty far out in the middle of no where not a single legit road for miles. The guys who were in charge of coming out and cleaning out the port potties was always behind schedule and lets just say the shit piles up quick.

But instructor port-potty only about 10 people used that one and really set the ambience for my blowjob I paid for in skittles. After I got my nut and she got cleaned up it was kind of awkward when we came out we kind of got caught by a Marine leaving the port potty's from his late night piss but I don't think he really was awake enough to care. We said our good byes and went our separate ways.

After that experience I decided Erin for some reason just wasn't someone I wanted to associate myself with anymore. Was is because she sucked my dick in the shitter? To answer that it would be no, I don't judge plus it was my dick and I wasn't a quarter of the asshole I was to become later down the road. But what really gave me the idea this girl is nasty vibes was seeing her feet. While in MCT we do about 4 or 5 hikes ranging from 3 miles to about 10 miles. At the end of a 10 mile hike your feet are rightfully fairly sore. What everyone does is take off there boots and socks. By no means it's a beautiful site or example of Marines at there finest. But fuck all of that bullshit my feet needed to breath. Looking around I see everyone and their nasty feet and I wasn't thinking much I had a apple eating it living my best life not a care in the world. I look over and see Erin's socks I swear on my dead goldfishes grave they were green.

    Those socks at one point were definitely brown but I later discovered she did not take her socks off once through the whole month. Just to give you a idea for the last month we have been walking at least a couple miles daily with full gear on which weighs about 60 pounds which doesn't sound like much but after wearing that all day it starts to add up. Imagine the type of sweat your socks accumulate from that. Let it be known I did not judge her for sucking my dick in a porta potty but I damn will judge you for being so lazy you wont take off your own dam socks for a month straight. Plus where

I went to next I didn't need to be held down by some girl with nasty feet.

When you get back from the field and complete all of your training you are blessed with a few hours of on base liberty. During this time you get your phone back and go to all the food places and stores on the base. There is one piece of advice I got from Sgt Sikes and still to this day credit him for me not being a complete ultimate boot. He told all of us prior to taking off "Everything over the last month I taught you take it or leave it. To be honest it really isn't going to be useful to most of you. But for the love of god don't go out and buy a stupid 100 plus dollar Marine camouflage backpack. It just looks ridiculous and you get a free one when you hit the fleet." At that exact moment I didn't quite get his point but if you have ever been to Oceanside, California or Jacksonville, North Carolina it doesn't take much to spot the boot Marines.

    Not really caring and just wanting to go call my parents and stuff my face with the

Wendy's on base we just nodded our heads and complied. After we get let go we was off like a herd of wild animals all walking as fast as we could toward where all the stores were trying to be first in line. The day MCT classes get liberty has to be the equivalent to black Friday shopping to all the stores. We come in there ready to blow away our last month of pay which adds up to about eight hundred bucks. When your there you start to notice the kids who have never really had money, they thought a couple hundred dollars was a small fortune. Luckily there is only so many things they could cram into there sweet brand new digital camouflage backpack. As I sit down and enjoy my baconator I quickly get what Sgt Sikes was talking about. I see about 100 Marines all with these needlessly large Marine Corps back packs on walking out of the PX (px is kind of like the target or Wal-Mart on base). The funniest thing about it is you could tell who bought what first. The first 20 to 30 came out with back packs matching our woodland green uniform. Then the second batch that showed up bit late

to the backpack party came out another 20 to 30 but these ones had a straight coyote brown backpacks and slightly more ridiculous looking. Then the last and most retarded of the boots come out and they have these bright desert color backpacks that don't go with there woodland uniform for shit. I sit there baconator in hand and realize these guys look completely retarded and wonder if they are aware of how dumb they look. Granted I did my fare share of many boot things the one thing I pride myself in is I never bought one of those stupid ass backpacks at MCT.
Remember the best Recruiter of the galaxy Dung? Through out the whole time from boot camp to the final couple hours before leaving MCT I still had no clue what my job was going to be. I asked around and after weeks of begging for an answer one of my instructors told me right before leaving I was Motor T. What is motor T you ask?

    Basically the bastard red headed stepchildren of the Marine Corps. Everyone in

Motor T are alcoholics at there finest. It's not the most glamorous job there is no real incentive. The work is shitty and your hands are dirty all the damn time. You work a shit ton in the field and garrison. We probably have more legal problems then anyone else except maybe infantry. But what we actually did was we fixed the shittest trucks you will ever see. That whole thing about adapting and overcoming is real easy when you got a few rolls of duct tape and JB weld. Being Motor T is when I really started my party days and It all begins right there over at Camp Johnson.

Chapter 4-Camp Johnson

Camp Johnson is seven miles up the road from where I just have been for the last month. At the time I had no real knowledge of what Jacksonville, North Carolina was like. When taking the bus up the road it seems like some very woodsy beautiful country. We come through the gate and as I come in I see these very new clean buildings. I thought to myself that this is going to be a great time. We drive past the nice buildings and ahead of us was some even more buildings not quite as nice but still fairly clean. I figure this is where I'm probably going it looks cool I'm about it.

We go right past those and there I see them. The barracks I was about to stay in for the next few months I shit you not have been around since the 1940s probably even older. You can see the roaches walking around outside like they owned the place. I thought to myself well fuck this is going to suck. We get off the bus and are greeted by this Corporal he is directing everyone where to put there bags what papers he needs and all that good stuff. I noticed he was the first Marine I have seen with an actual full set of hair. It doesn't sound like much but being bald and having a quarter inch of hair just on the top of your head, its gets cold after a while. Cpl long hair starts sorting us off into our rooms by threes. I head into my room with these other three we are told to be outside ready to go by 0600. It's currently like 1700, which is 5pm. I for the first time in the Marines have legit time off. We all get settled into this room and they start changing into regular clothes.

My first boot mistake when packing all my uniforms I didn't even throw one pair of jeans and shirt into my bags. We decided to go check out the dominos on base. As we make our way over there I notice I am not the only one who made the same mistake of not bringing regular clothes. We go splurge and eat way to many pieces of pizza and head back.

Waking up earlier for the most part on your own is really odd at first after being yelled at to wake up and hurry up for the last four months. All of our alarms went off at 0515. I sit up looking around expecting to get yelled at and nothing. I stretch my arms and legs and slowly wiggle out from bed. We take our turns shaving and using the sink. Its 0545 and we are all outside because we was warned 15 minutes prior was a super important thing in the Marines. Imagine this its 5:45am in the morning in the beginning of winter its about 30 degrees and we have nothing of warmth on because well we are dumb boots and no one told us to wear a sweat shirt underneath our uniform. At around 0555 Corporal long hair comes out his room barely awake wearing all the sweat shirts and sweat pants. He reads off everyone's names making sure we are there. He gets done then said " go get breakfast be back here at 7:30".

Confused as hell we all head off to the chow hall wondering what do we do with all this time. Marine Corps chow halls are not the best eating establishments but the food is okay. They take about 350 dollars out of your paycheck every month for it regardless if you go or not but that's beside the point. There is one thing these chow halls exceed at and only one thing and that is making omelets. I shit you not they will serve rare chicken and fish without a care in the world for your health. But they put the most time and effort into your omelets in the morning its equal to a premier breakfast establishment. After devouring our breakfast we had back to our dirty little barracks building and are waiting for it to be 7:30. I'm out in the smoke pit and where my habit of smoking begins. One of the guys I'm talking to notices I'm not smoking and offers me one of his Marlboro Reds. At this point the only time I have smoked was before I went to boot camp and even then I didn't actually inhale them at all. I take one of his cigarettes and light it up. I blow the smoke out and he informs me I have to inhale the smoke. I try it again this time inhaling it properly I start to cough my lungs out just like anyone who inhales a Marlboro red for the first time. When I'm done coughing I get this buzz much like the one I got from dipping at boot camp. I really liked it plus it warmed me up a lot, which I enjoyed even more.

At this point checking in is quite the breeze you walk around, you give people papers, answer some questions smile and be nice. Life lesson I learnt just from watching the same people do the same thing over and over again when your nice to someone they genuinely are more helpful with your situation and if need to will go a little bit out of their job for you. But when you're a dick or just very yes or no, no small talk they take what you give. We get informed later that day which building we are moving to. Camp Johnson for job training is split up in to three schools. You got Supply they are basically our version of amazon. They have the newest building right by the gate with all the recreational centers you could imagine. There school is about a month long and they pick up class immediately.

Next is Administration school. Just like the name implies they deal with all the paper work Marines come with and making sure our pay is good. They had the other nicer barracks I saw earlier. Their school is two weeks long and they pick up immediately. Last but not least is the Motor Transport barracks they are the oldest barely livable building on base. Our school is three months long and it takes up to 3 plus months just to start a class.

Packing up everything you own and moving is second nature at this point. I have all my stuff loaded up on my back, shoulders, and front of my body. I walk about 50 yards from where the barracks I just moved into yesterday to my new home for the next 6 months. I am greeted by a Staff Sergeant and handed a key he explains where my room is and I'm off the second deck room 14. I unlock the door and notice no one is there I immediately drop my stuff on a bottom bed. I scope the room and see four beds. There is three closet size lockers to the side. We have two sinks both work condition and a bathroom with a toilet and shower in it. Shortly after I'm checking the room out, my roommate Bruce Banner greets me. I have seen him around at boot camp and MCT but have never had a conversation with him. Bruce is a little bit older then me, had a fiancé, and is from

Tennessee. I didn't know at the time but me and Bruce was going to be with each other for the next three years having a very up and down friendship. At the end of the day he became my brother. Then my next roommate was Loki. If there were someone that would have my back it would be Bruce. If there was someone that would fuck me over it would be Loki. Obviously I had no idea at the time he was a worm but at the time I thought he was going to a great friend.

As Bruce and Loki get there bed situation worked out we get called outside. We come out and get sorted into our classes. There are about 15 classes from the most senior class at the front of line down to us being the most junior class. Each class has a class leader it's usually just the oldest Marine Student in the class. For mine it was this guy named Hernandez he was 23, let's just say he was a goofball and could be quite the douche at times. But in retrospect considering he had to deal with about 15 Marines all about 18-20 and was just as new to the Marines as us he wasn't that bad. A lot of our days were spend standing as a big group of 15 classes all with 15-20 Marines in each one. We would all march from the barracks to the chow hall. From there back to the barracks and then to school every single day.

When getting 300 people all together and moving its always a bit of a process.

Anyway back to where we just came outside we are in our group and get told we have a piss test. For my very short career everywhere I had been they make you have a canteen to drink water from at all times. With my slight increase in freedom I had not drank water at all that day. They let us all walk off to get water and start lining up around the outside of the barracks to prepare for our piss test. This is where I discover I am part camel. After several hours everyone has finished the piss test except yours truly. I stand over the toilet with my piss bottle in hand trying my best and nothing comes out. The Marine in charge of the piss test tells me if I cant pee there are going to stick a needle in my penis and extract the urine that way. Obviously he is full of shit but I didn't know that.

I go back to the toilet and have an idea! I tell him I'm going to poop so that way I can squeeze my piss out. He realizes the mistake he made scaring me like that. I sit down while staring at this Marine I start to squeeze and sure enough I filled up the bottle. I finish up and the Marine that just watched me poop just to make myself piss in a bottle refuses to look at me. I come and turn my bottle in, grinning ear to ear happy as hell I'm not having a needle up my penis today.

While waiting to get into the class rotation to start doing our job is a lot of "stand by" which is just a fancy word for sitting around you barracks all day. Since I was doing that I fount out my mailing address and payed my father to next day ship all of my clothes and video games. Since I wasn't like most of the other boots I still had quite a bit of money saved up from boot camp and MCT so I figured it wouldn't hurt getting comfortable real quick. By Thursday of my first week I was nice and settled in I bought a TV from a guy that was graduating and fount computer speakers by the dumpster that worked perfectly. We had these small office style lockers called secretary's and mine was by far the most decked out. During Stand by time my roommates and me would chill spend a lot of our days watching movies and playing video games. But that all changed when Friday came. On Fridays we were released for the weekends but we had to be back in formation at midnight. It was called Cinderella liberty. For these midnight formations we didn't have to be in uniform or even sober for the most part. It was a bit of a competition who would be the drunkest Marine.

One thing about the Marine Corps and there demographic for jobs is majority of female Marines are two jobs Supply or Admin. Both of which had nicer barracks and were within walking distance of our rat infested barracks. Luckily I had one friend that we went back to boot camp with named Will Brownstein. He was my in over at the supply barracks. I hit him up and since I didn't really know my roommates yet decided to go alone. I headed over there and meet up with Will and ask him how it is over here tells me he has the same set up with midnight as us. We go outside and there is this big group of females all drinking and partying it up and gathered around the grill like it's a bonfire. We go scope it out and there kind of bitches.

    At the time Will and me were only 19 so getting alcohol was a bit of a challenge and we had no adult to buy it for us. Since they were on the more ghetto darker side I decide we pull the robbery. While Will is bugging them I sneak around and put there bottle of grey goose in my pants. They finally tell him to fuck off and I give him the green light that we are good. Having a bottle of grey goose in your pants is pretty easy for the guy in charge of the barracks for the night to spot and for Will's barracks there is only one way in. But for mine there was multiple entry points due to it being outside so we decide lets go to my room. We manage to sneak into my room without anyone noticing and I see Bruce curled up in bed talking to his fiancé. That is where he spent most of his time. Then Loki sitting on top of his bed reading what I think was book. I look at them both and ask who wants to turn up Bruce rolls over and Loki looks like we made his night. One thing I forgot to steal from them was chasers. But us being young and dumb we decided lets drink it straight. Fast forward two hours we are completely annihilated and we go outside and wobble downstairs to the smoke pit. This is where smoking started becoming fun it's where you do all your networking and met a bunch of other people all just as drunk as us. We start talking about what's fun to get into on the weekend. They all talk about the supply and admin barracks. Then someone sitting down wearing an Asian bathrobe and cowboy boots calmly said "La Mirage".

At that time it was getting very close to midnight and everyone was making there way outside for formation. I turn around and the man in the bathrobe is gone. I don't think much about it but that word driftwood stayed in my head. We walk over and stand in our assigned class. Will has run off back to his barracks and it's me and Loki standing next to a guy named McMeans. Now

Loki and me were drunk but McMeans just turned 21 a few days earlier this week, safe to say he was beyond drunk.

Time goes by and we have been standing there for a while. It's very cold and we start to get very anxious. I start to hear this dripping. I look to my left and this drunk bastards McMeans is pissing in the middle of formation right on the shoes of the guy in front of him. He jumps out of the way fast as hell and goes to grab him by the kneck. Hernandez being the baby sitter he was forced to be manages to pull him off and during this whole time McMeans didn't break a stream of his piss off. At this point Loki and me are laughing our Asses off and just can't control ourselves. Hernandez keeps telling us to shut up but we can't stop. Just as McMeans manages to put his dick back in his pants the Ssgt in charge of getting a count of everyone walks up and ask us what is so funny. When you're underage and drunk and a superior makes direct eye contact with you it's the most sobering thing on the planet. Me and Loki stiff up like perfect statues and reply with "nothing SSgt". He takes our counts and we get released to bed. Loki and me decide we have had enough fun for our first Friday night in the school house and call it a night.

Saturday I slept in for the first time since I went home on boot camp leave. It felt so amazing waking up at 10am. The only bad part is I missed breakfast at the chow hall. Loki and me decide to go to the Px and grab some food. On our way there we run in to a guy in our class named Jared Vasconseles. I didn't remember but he said we was talking to him a lot last night out in the smoke pit before formation. I vaguely remember him but just trying to be friendly we let him tag along on our walk to the store. We get there and I purchase a pack of those Marlboro Reds I tried a few times. After we load up with an excessive amount of junk food we head back to the barracks. Dan, Jared, and I are sitting watching TV.

While sitting there we get to talk and decide we want to hit up the town of Jacksonville. We start asking how do we get off base and remembered there's a parking lot by the chow hall full of taxis. We walk over and sure enough there is about 10 dirty looking ford crown vics out there with dirty smelly drivers to match. In the time before uber you had no real choice on how to get around you either took a cab or didn't go anywhere. We ask the cab driver where is somewhere fun to go he snarl "just git in da dam car". Disregarding what our parents taught us we hop in the car with this stranger and we are off. Driving out the gate and into Jacksonville I should have noticed something. Every building was a barbershop, tattoo parlor, or a run down hotel. Not having much freedom so far as an adult I take it in happily as hell. Then we get to the probably the biggest building in the town and possibly the cleanest building the Mall. This mall is often referred to many as the boot mall. As I walk in I start to see them. These cliché 2012 boots are out in full force they all wear for the most part the same outfit uniform issued boots, bloused blue jeans, tactical tan uniform belt, Green t-shirt, dog tags visible on neck, raging high and tight haircut, and last but not least PX issued MCT backpack with excessive amount of things stored in it. For every normal customer in this mall you see there is about 10 of the exact described person I just mentioned. We walk around and start checking out the stores and these shops know how to make sells I discovered real quickly. We go into a hat store and are greeted by this girl about our age and pretty attractive Loki being the horn dog he is starts flirting with her right away and she plays this man like a fiddle at the end of it he spent like 200 dollars on hats.

As we are walking around we decide to stop by the food court and grab some food. We start talking about what we should get into tonight and It comes back to me the word the guy from the night before said "La Mirage". We look it up and discover it is a gentleman's club. We all laugh at the idea and decide lets head back to base. Luckily cab drivers are at every single spot us boot Marines go and we head back this time in a lot cleaner vehicle.

As we pull up to the barracks its right around late afternoon time frame and this is where barracks shenanigans are at their highest. There is nerfgun firefights going on the walkways and people rolling around in rolling chairs just acting like 5 year olds. As we walk up we run into this guy named Yarbrough getting shot by all these nerf guns, he is this really goofy guy that was not meant for our job and has been at our school for the last nine months. He ask us if we ever heard about four lokos and at the time all I knew was they has alcohol in them. He told us in the middle of this nerf gun war if we need some he sells them 10 bucks a pop. Looking back that dude made a killing off us. After getting lit up by nerf guns Jared goes back to his room Loki and Me head to ours. We come in and Bruce is right where he was when we left in the same corner of his bed on his phone. Loki and me decide to go onto this website called omegle. It's pretty much dudes flashing there dicks, but every now and then you met a girl that is of age. It was here I met Jasmine Lopez.

The Story of Jasmine Lopez is what set me on the pathway of douche bag fuck boy Marine. As me and Loki are clicking through the herds of guys showing there dicks on omelet we come across this girl she look cute and seems nice enough. We start talking and I hit off with her really well. Turns out she actually lives in Jacksonville, North Carolina. I thought wow this girl is my in she said she is about to buy a car in a couple weeks and would love to pick me up from base. All the danger signs I should have saw right away went completely over my head. I "dated" her for about two months. It turns out Jasmine worked at an establishment called La Mirage. There was a lot strip clubs in Jacksonville the two powerhouses being La Mirage and Driftwood. Dating a stripper is a hard lesson having to learn, especially one in a military town they are about 10 times more mentally fucked up then your average stripper. Regardless I think being with a $stripper$ is going to be awesome she will always have money, get me free drinks, and get VIP treatment when I come to visit her. While it started with everything I wanted it ended pretty badly.

We started talking, video chatting, and texting for a couple weeks. Friday afternoon she tells me to come to her strip club and bring some friends. I bring Will and Loki and we head to the strip club via shitty cab. It cost exactly 12.00 from chow hall of camp Johnson to La Mirage its perfect because it's easy to split that up no matter how many people you bring. We get the Club and I inform the bouncer I'm friends with Jasmine the dude gives me a strange look rolls his eyes and shakes his head as he said "come on in". We get through and I see the strip club to the left and a bar right next to that is the main dance stage, in the back is a dark hallway, which leads to the private rooms. Jasmine and I make eye contact and I get a really nervous feeling in my stomach and we say hi to each other and she starts making all the stripper moves on me. We sit down with her on my lap, she ask "you want a drink honey". I told her I'm only 19 and she replied, "That's not what I asked". I realize where she is getting at so I ask her well jack and coke sounds good. I pay her $20 damn dollars for a jack and coke. She goes and gets it all my friends think I'm cool as hell. She comes back and I start drinking.

A few hours go by we are all having a good time nice and liquored up Jasmine ask me to get a dance so we can go back into the private rooms. I go to the atm and pull out about 200 dollars and we go back. She sits me down closes the door and starts to do her private dance routine. Then she starts taking off my pants she literally has my dick in her hand and is breathing on it and ask me do I want to keep going. At this point I am a drunk, horny, 19 year old of course I would do anything. I reply "yes baby" she tells me I'm going to need to fork over another $100. I without skipping a beat hand it over immediately.

Not realizing I technically just solicited for prostitution she starts giving me my first blowjob and I coincidently got my first case of whiskey dick. This girl earned all $100 dollars she was there for about 15 minutes doing her best and I just wasn't budging my dick basically was covered in Novocain. I feel kind of bad but her being the crazy stripper she was thought it was more of a challenge. As I put my whiskey dick away and head back outside I realize holy shit it's like 11:55. It takes about 10 minutes to get to base. I gather up all my boys and head outside and there is no cabs outside. We are freaking out we have no way to get back to base and Bruce texts us saying "Hey where are you guys? We are starting to form up?" We are franticly trying to call ever Cab Company in Jacksonville begging for anyone to come get us. Every Cab company was saying it's going to be about ten minutes. We are fearing the worst getting in trouble this early in your career they will just kick you out immediately without thinking about it. Just as all hope is almost lost a Marine walks out and sees us freaking out.

The Marine ask us "You guys are on Johnson huh"? We reply, "Yes how do you know?" He said "yea been there before its almost midnight shouldn't you be back at base by now?"

We get talking and he agrees to take us back to the barracks for $40. We have no option but him so we take it. We pulled up at 12:06 right outside the barracks where we form up at. Will Sprints to his barracks then Loki and me sneak around back? As they guy in charge says the first names I pull up as he said my name. While completely gassed and out of breath I spurt out "Huur". And lean down on my hands and knees trying to hold my vomit in. He gets through our class and about 2 seconds after he leaves my class I proceed to vomit into the dirt below me.

I successfully manage to get through formation and head back to my room. I look like a complete mess I'm drunk, have vomit on my shirt, and look like I just ran a marathon in jeans and t-shirt. When I get back to the room Bruce gives us the disappointed father look and proceeds back to his bed. I get cleaned up and decide the party should continue. Jasmine still is working so I don't think much about her at the moment and remember we need some booze. I remember Yarbrough being the plug for 4 lokos, I head to his room. I knock on his door and he is standing there plastered as hell and greets me "hey yo watt up man". I ask him if he has any four lokos and he responds "yo of course man I hope you like orange cause that's all I got" He then gives me the best advice for drinking these "no matter who you are how much you drink prior all it takes is two at the most". I kept with that rule for the rest of my tenure of the school house. We get out loaded up and smuggle them back to our rooms. We spend the rest of the night drinking and smoking deciding when we would go back to La Mirage.

I wake up the next morning with about 20 missed phone calls and about 50 text messages from Jasmine. She is mad obviously I didn't hit her up for the rest of the night. I agree to take to the movies and see one of those twilight movies that was in theaters at the time. We meet up outside the movies and go see it. I don't really remember watching the movie to be honest I just remember a lot of foreplay throughout the whole thing. Afterwards we leave and she insists we get a hotel room and I agree we head to one of the most premier hotels in Jacksonville. The old Comfort Inn. It was where most Marines go during the weekend to party. We get checked in and as we were walking to the room she grabs my junk. We are practically having sex before we even get in the room. I manage to open the door and we go in barely closing it on the way in. As we get to beating cheeks she starts to do some of the craziest shit I've only seen in porn at this point she manages to grab my hips and flip herself into a position so we are doing a standing 69. Only problem with that position it tires you out really quick. So I proceed to throw her onto the bed and go straight to doggy style pounding guts loud enough so the next three rooms had to hear it. We wrap up and lay down completely exhausted on both ends.

We wake up from our nap after a couple hours decide to have a round two wasn't as intense as the first one but got my nut regardless then we decide to go get food. Conveniently enough there was a waffle house right across the street and we go eat there. We talk about how this relationship is going to work moving forward. She explains she is about to buy a car and if I was willing to help out with the payments she wouldn't mind picking me up all the time. This at the time should have been a major red flag but all I thought was hey no more shitty taxis. We agree that I will give her 300 dollars a month for her car. It was a 2003 Mercedes C230 not a bad car but no way in hell her payments was anywhere close to 300 bucks.

A few more weeks go by and it seems like I have the perfect system on Fridays Jasmine comes and gets me; I give her money at the strip club. She uses that money to get our hotels each weekend it seems like a perfect arrangement. Then eventually I had the ups comes the downs. Remember all of my "standy by" time? Well we finally get a date to start class and we are pretty excited as a group. What does that mean? Well my days of being able to talk to her during the daytime was decreased significantly due to having to go to school and was learning how to be a Motor T mechanic. Another thing we started getting was homework in the beginning and didn't know how to BS it real quick. One weekend when we were supposed to do our arrangement, I informed her I couldn't go out because we had to study for out test. Let's just say she did not like that one bit. This is where the crazy stripper side started to come out she called and harassed me the whole weekend detailing how she was going to fuck me up and destroy everything I owned. At first I didn't think much due to being on a military base how can she come get me anyway I'm safe. Right? Then I remembered how the hell has she been able to pick me up every Friday without me getting her through the gate? I started to get worried then.

Saturday night I get a text saying I'm in the parking lot come out. I start freaking out asking my roommates how the hell did this happen. They basically told me I either got to handle it or tell the guy in charge of the barracks to call the Military Police. I walk outside and she looks like a hot mess she has mascara running down her face from crying and just look like a beat puppy. She slaps me in the face not hard by any means it could almost be described as playful. She sobbing in my arms how she misses me and can't be away from me. This was my first experience dealing with a level 5 clinger stripper edition. I console her and agree Sunday we would go out. Before she leaves she ask me for the car payment. Not thinking much of it we drive over to the store where the ATM is and I pull out $300 and give it to her. This is my first time being played like a fiddle without realizing it.

A few more weeks go by and it's November and my birthday is coming up and it landed on a Friday. At this point I was pretty good friends with most of my class. We decide to have a party in the barracks and my neighbor next door his name is Tony Stark. We ended up becoming best friends later on but at this point we just had mutual friends and was cool with each other. I get the green light from Jasmine to hang out with the boys in the barracks and everything is going great. We are playing beer pong, shot gunning beers, and taking shots. We had some of the females from supply and admin over and of course they are getting slutty. It gets announced it's my birthday and one of them takes it upon her to give me a lap dance. At this point I am a professional lap dance receiver and nothing really budges me due to who I was dating. It was a great time even Bruce left his bed and came partied with us for a bit. Time goes by and this supply girl whose name I don't even remember starts to get real intimate with me. Being the drunk guy I was whispered to her to take my key and go back to my room ill be there in a bit. I did this so that way no one would really notice what we were about to do. A lot of the guys went to La mirage and couldn't have them telling Jasmine.

She leaves and I go and tell Bruce and Loki my game plan. Bruce rolls his eyes tells me" just because it's your birthday Ill go sleep in someone else's room tonight. Then when I told Loki he said, "You do you I'm just going to go to sleep". Just before I'm about to make my exit we get a very loud knock on the door. If you know what it sounds like when the police knock on the door you understand that feeling of your gut just dropping like your about to fall. We freak out the girls hide in the bathroom we put the booze away and open the door. Sure enough it's the SSgt on duty for the night. He smells the alcohol on our underage breath and ask whose party this is. This is where I respected Stark he said without missing a beat "this party was my idea and my doing". I realized the type of trouble he might be in I came in and said "Its my birthday SSgt this was a lot of my doing as well". Let it be known he could have done a lot worse punishment to us then he did which I'm thankful to this day, but at the time it still sucked. He had us take all the alcohol out of our room and watched us pour it all outside on the dirt. While doing that he started naming off all of his Friends that have died. When we got done with all of that he told us to be down stairs in Cammies at 0600 Saturday morning ready to work. We agree and head back to our rooms.

I come back I see that female I told to go in my room watching TV. I look at her and decide fuck it and I proceeded to try and fuck her in my bed. The problem with military bunk beds is there is not a lot of clearance so I kept hitting the top and it was made of sheet metal so it kept making this loud booming sound. I decide to just do her on the carpet. One piece of advice for fucking on the carpet put a blanket down or something if not you will suffer the worse rug burn on your knees. As I was destroying my knees I finally manage to cum I look at her and feel pretty greasy. I think she felt the same way as well, because we didn't say bye or even look at each other afterwards she just got dressed and left. I look up at Loki and he said sarcastically "how was your birthday man?" I tell him to fuck off as I put my underwear on and roll into bed.

Chapter- 5 Christmas and New years

I wake up to my door getting banged on at 0545. I open it and there's Stark he looks me with the most annoyed face and yells "Get the fuck ready fool". I mumble, "Oh shit yea I'm on it". I get ready as fast as possible and we head downstairs to check in with the duty. As I walk in there stands the Ssgt on duty and our class leader Hernandez and he looks pisses rightfully so. The Ssgt ask if we know what we were about to do and of course we respond with a 'no Ssgt". He smiles and calmly said, "Today you boys are going to be making the base beautiful". I looked at him confused as hell and discover basically we was doing bitch work all day. To give you the idea imagine the area we was collecting trash was about the size of average mall to include the parking lot loading areas and etc. We spent a little over 12 hours bending over picking every piece of trash around this part of the base. When we finally got done and came back to see the Ssgt He told us he could have reported us made us lose our E-2 rank and pay(that we just got like 17 days ago) be confined to the barracks for 45 days, and not go home for the holidays. I wont every forget this man then he said this "I'm not going to punish your Mother and Father for your dumb actions, I'm going to let you go home for Christmas but you bet your ass you will be here for New Years". In hind sight that's what a good leader and man would do you don't see that much in todays military.

We nod our heads and thank him for showing mercy on us. The days to Christmas are getting closer and Jasmine and me have grown very distant. I started realizing how much money she is taking from me and start to ghost her slowly. Then came the part where I grew a bit of a brain and cut her off. One day after school she was blowing up my phone. During this time we did PT after class since it was so cold in the morning. I see her calling me as I'm changing into my running suit and I ignore her. I go out and run with my class for about 30-45 minutes we get back, get told what the plan is for tomorrow and we are released for the day.

I go grab to go dinner and head to my room. I see she sent me a picture it's her car with all her tires slashed. She has several messages saying I did this and I was going to jail and etc. I call her and all she said was "hope your ready for jail bitch" and proceeds to hang up. Luckily where this dumb bitch fucked up is trying to frame someone whose has multiple people confirm where he is through out the day. The reported incident was believed to happen somewhere between 1pm and 6pm on a Wednesday. Luckily when she gave the police my name and where I worked it was shut down pretty quick due to it being very easy to prove where I was at during those hours. But of course I had to go and talk to the people in charge again and coincidentally I had to talk to the same Ssgt who already saved my ass before. He looked at me with a face that can only be described as what the fucking fuck man. I give him a look that your dog gives after he pisses in the house. He then laughs and said "Soo you gotta thing for strippers huh beach? "I look at him confused and go "how do you know she is a stripper Ssgt?" He laughs and goes "been there done that have the shirt" the rest of the Staff around the office start to laugh. He tells me La mirage might not be the best place for me to go anymore and he can't force me not to go but recommends if I have to have my stripper fix I should start visiting Driftwood.

As holiday season approaches they shut down school and everyone starts purchasing plane tickets from a few days before Christmas to a few days after New Year's. Due to my deal with Ssgt who saved my ass I could only go between the 23rd and had to be back the 26th. I appreciated what he had but it was going to cost me over $1000 dollars and just didn't seem worth it. I make up some bullshit excuse to my parents why I can't come home for the Christmas and prepare to sit at the barracks and watch movies.

The day comes and everyone leaves for the holidays Its just me and a few other people left like maybe 20 or so from the whole entire school. The only other guy from my class was Jared Vasconseles. We start hanging out and a he tells me he has some friends that are down in Myrtle Beach visiting from Texas. Since there was no formation during these 4 days off we looked at bus tickets from Jacksonville to Myrtle Beach. They cost only $60 bucks each. I end up spotting Jared because he was broke. We pack our stuff get a hotel booked and head to the bus station. It was a beautiful scenery on the way down to Myrtle Beach. We get checked in and check where the girls from Texas are they said they needed money to get over there. I go to a western union and wire them about $500. They end up saying there staying home for Christmas but will come out for new years and we agree that's cool.

Jared and me get to our hotel in Myrtle Beach and what's the first thing we look up? Strip Clubs obviously. We find one that will even come pick you up in a red limo. We call them and he pulls up in this old as Buick limo. We hop in and this ghetto black dude named Troy greets up and tells us was sup and shows us were the mini bar is and we are off. We pull up to the strip club and go through feeling like rock stars. Here we meet this two strippers one was a blond girl and the other a black girl can't remember their names but is was Christmas Eve and we were all lonely. This wasn't a premier place like La mirage it was the type of strip club where the strippers are getting hammered on the clock. We all get hammered until closing time and then Troy comes in and tells us its time to go home. The strippers end up coming with us. We get back to our hotel and proceed to bang the shit out of these strippers. We swapped them, we tag teamed them, and fucked in every position under the sun. It wasn't the proudest moment in my life but hey Merry Christmas to me.

I wake up the next morning and they are both gone. I have a weird feeling I should check my wallet. Sure enough the $200 dollars I had was gone. I kind of figured that would have happened but didn't think of hiding my wallet while having sex with these sluts. We decided to stay in the hotel that day and watch Christmas story and call our parents to try and even out all the dirty things that have happened the night prior.

We wrap up all our phone calls and talk to the Jared's friend from Texas their Names was Kaley and Shelbi. We talk to them and they tell us they are leaving there house and are headed to South Carolina. We relax and patiently start waiting for them to arrive. We make up a cover story about our whole weekend and basically make it sound like we been baking cookies and building ginger bread houses and not tag teaming strippers.

They arrived around noon the next day. They made great time and were grinding on the road I give them kudos for that. We finally meet Kaley and me hit it off the only weird thing was she was 27 and had a kid. I didn't think much of it at least she wasn't a stripper. Jared and me decide to drive back to Jacksonville since they have been driving from Texas they could use the break. We get there and head to the barracks so we could change get some new clothes and head to the hotel we just booked for new years.

When we go into the barracks seeing Loki in the room surprises me. We say hello talk a little bit he tells me about his Christmas and so on. I tell him about the girls we had waiting on us in the car and he tells us to hit him up later so we can all party. I agree grab my clothes Jared and I are on our way to the hotel. We get checked in and since Kaley was 27 we had her buy a shit ton of alcohol. Like enough to last me the rest of my time aboard Camp Johnson. We go back to the hotel and start turning up. Most of my sexual encounters have been pretty fun for the most part.

Kaley was the first example of fucking a dead fish. I shit you not no matter what I did she just layed there and did nothing. I don't know if I was just a bad lay or what but nothing I did was working for her. I look over and Shelby was going to town on Jared but I wasn't trying to treat them like strippers. Being a good person I stuck with my dead fish and got my nut. We get done and get ready for bed. I realized Shelby was a freak that night. While we was all sleeping she tried to get Jared to do a round 2 but he was out like a log. She then came to my bed and tried starting a three-way but just like Jared Kaley aka dead fish was out. Me and her then went into the bathroom and decided to fuck like rabbits. It got so Smokey in there from our hot ass breathes you would have sworn we were taking a hot shower. Towards the end remembering I had no condom on I pulled out at the last second and took one expert shot right into the toilet I hit it perfectly, I was very proud of myself, even Shelby complimented me on my aim. We laughed for a little bit swore we wouldn't tell the other two about this and went back to sleep.

We wake up the next morning it's the night before New Year's Eve. We go out to the boot mall and Kaley was being very distant I didn't really care but figured I should show some emotion considering I just paid for her to come all the way out here from Texas. I ask what she wants to do and get nothing so I take her to Chuckie cheese because I figured can't be negative there. We win a whole bunch of tickets and end up giving them to some kid it was a great time but yet she is being weird and distant. We go to Walmart and I even buy her kid some toy to try and cheer her up nothing. The day goes on I start to give up on trying to make her happy. We end up back at the hotel to drink and party into the New Year and Kaley decided to keep being the dealfish so I invited Loki over. We start drinking and being typical drunk me I ask Kaley what's up. She goes into detail how she really likes me and just doesn't want to go back home and be with me forever. I for the first time actually feel like I have someone I can connect with and I assure her when I figure out where I'm going to be stationed at I would bring her out there immediately. We rejoice and everything seems amazing. Loki comes over with a few other guys from the barracks and we are drinking playing beer pong and for the first time in a long time I actually feel at peace with the universe. I start to get a little dizzy drunk later in the night and I remember Loki saying something along the lines he was going to rent the room next door. The hotel had the door where you could join both the rooms together so it was even more fun as the night went on somehow my shoes ended up in his room. I end up laying in bed dizzy and super drunk. The last thing I remember was looking into Kaley's eyes.

I wake up I look around I'm empty in the bed and the hotel room is a complete mess. I see Jared and Shelby asleep in the bed next to me and a couple guys on the floor. I look at the door that joined our hotel rooms together its closed and locked on Dan's side. At first I didn't think anything about it. I'm really thirsty at this point and went outside to buy a Gatorade from the vending machine but can't find my shoes for the life of me. I remember they are in the other room and say fuck it and head to the vending machine barefoot. As I get my Gatorade and head back up I stop and think where the fuck is Kaley. I have that sick feeling in my gut and start to try and play it off in my head. No way Loki would fuck her I just told him last night that we really like each other and want to be a real relationship. Kaley wouldn't fuck him she just confessed her true feeling for me. At this point any logically person would know where this is going I head up to Loki's hotel room and start banging on the door. No answer. I bang on it some more still no answer. I look through the window and see someone move into the bathroom. I start banging on the door again and Kaley finally answers the door. She instantly had the look of guilt on her face. I ask her with s straight face "did you?" She never responded. I went in the room fount my shoes and got a cab straight back to Camp Johnson.

The rest of the day my phone was getting blown up by everyone Jared, Dan, and Kaley. I decided to ignore them all go the the recreational center on base and play pool. It was there I ran into Tony Stark. We said hello and started playing against each other. I shared with him the story and we made a pretty big joke of it. After about 6 plus hours of them calling me I finally decided to answer one of Kaley calls. This bitch had the audacity to tell me if I wasn't going to spend time with her she at least needed money to head back to Texas. I told her to go fuck herself and Loki could give her the money.

The funny part was Loki spent his last bit of money on that hotel room and somehow Jared was always broke so he couldn't give them money to get home. To this day I'm not sure exactly how they got back home but I can tell you one thing for certain it was not through my money. I ended up making amends with Loki realizing bros before hoes and we both agreed she was a dead fish anyway. The good news is we still had all the liquor we had her buy and Loki brought it all back to our room. Only problem was alcohol in the barracks was being cracked down on. Being the mischievous kids we were decided to hide all our cheap vodka bottles in a trash bag above our ceiling tiles.

Chapter 6- The end of Camp Johnson

A few weeks after all of the Christmas and new years events had past and I have decided to cut out my partying I take up my new favorite hobby annoying the shit out of Bruce. As I have stated before Bruce liked to spend the majority of his time curled up in bed talking to his fiancé her name is Natasha. Natasha actually during that time gave me a lot of good advice from the women perspective. Due to our living situation she knew the whole story of my life over the last couple months and all the women I have had ups and downs with. One day as Loki and Me were sitting in Bruce's bed much to his discontent Natasha told me over facetime "you look a lot happier when you're not messing around with all of those women you should try and dedicate more time to your guy friends". I really took that to heart. I decided to take that to heart and start doing that and it really helped me develop as a young man.

Now that I started staying on base a lot more Bruce started to get out of bed a lot more. We would frequently go over to the recreational center and play pool we even had a cook out one of our weekends. For the first time in a long time everything was at harmony in my life. That was until I heard the Dogs one early Saturday morning.

It was early as hell one Saturday morning, I was woke up to people running along the walkways and banging on doors. I still with my eyes closed stumble to the door and open it. As I wipe my eyes and barely open the door there I see, 100s of Marines outside from all around the other barracks buildings. There was several Military police with dogs at every corner possible and was flat out chaotic as hell. I start hearing screams "get dressed and head down stairs now!!" Bruce, Loki, and me throw some sweat pants and hoodies on we try and pick up the room real quick make it somewhat presentable because we have an idea where this is going.

We get down stairs and run through the process of a normal formation getting all of our numbers for each class routed up through the chain of command. We ask Hernandez the class leader what is going on. He obviously knows something was up but he decided to ignore us like a douche.
We had to be standing there for at least an hour or so the sun had already rose and my legs are becoming very stiff. The

instructors from our course come out and ask us if we have anything in the barracks we shouldn't have? My heart stops for about two seconds. I remember all of those liquor bottles I have stored above the ceiling in my barracks room. I look over at Bruce and Loki and they give me a look that can only be described as we are fucked.

Next thing is we all go stand right outside the doors to our barracks and that's when the dogs started coming through. I see about five of them at the end of my walkway each dog going into a separate room. I hear one bark and immediately followed by two Marines being escorted into the room. I didn't personally know who it was but I would see them down the road later. The dogs get closer and closer to our room.

At this point I'm sweating bullets and have no idea if they are checking ceilings. I knew there was no way a dog could smell a closed bottle of alcohol but it attributed to the stress and had all three of us on edge. The dogs and Military police come in and start walking around the room. While outside I hear them say something. I felt like I was sneaking drugs through customs or something. I hear them mumbling and I have that feeling like I'm falling off a chair. After what felt like an eternity they come out and move on to the next room. The biggest feeling of relief came over all of us and we all looked at each other without saying a single word but our expressions said it all we just dodged a fucking bullet.

We have now been up for about 4 hours on a Saturday morning and the dogs and military police finally was all gone. Then we all went straight back out into the field right next to the barracks. I saw a man walk over he was quite a bit older then all of us. I knew he was important by the way all of our instructors got very stiff and were being more professional then usual. He comes out and has all of us sit down on the wet shitty grass/dirt. He lifts in his hand a bottle of Southern Comfort which is a brand of liquor. At this point there seemed to be incidents every weekend and sure as shit they all involve alcohol. The event that caused the highest ranking Marine on the base to come down and have the barracks searched was pretty bad. This isn't my story I had no part in any of it or do I condole any of it. The summary is along the lines two male Marines got two female Marines blacked out drunk proceeded to sexually assault them then at the end threw them both into the shower and turned on the water to wake them up. The females ended up needing to get rushed to the hospital to get there stomachs pumped. After hearing this story rightfully so the base commander took it upon himself to ensure the barracks were completely dry. After he proceeded to tell us how disgusting these actions were and how the Marines at fault would be receiving maximum punishments. He stated any alcohol incident from here out he would oversee the punishment personally.

After all of that was said and done I was beyond scared. I didn't want to take the bottles out due to someone seeing me with them. But I had no idea what to do with all those bottles of cheap liquor. What did I do you might ask? Nothing I did absolutely nothing and 8 years later those bottles might still be in the barracks room for all I know.

Around Thursday of that next week we get pulled out of class and pulled into the bay where all the trucks we practice working on are located. It's pretty large area enough to fit about a dozen or more trucks. Today though the bay was completely empty and only thing in there was single portable table with a foldable chair and some papers on it. We start sitting on the floor by groups with a walkway leading straight the table being clear. A little while later after all of us are sitting the base commander walks in. When a high ranking officer steps into a building to announce his presence we call attention on deck.

Which is followed by all of us standing at the position of attention till he directs us otherwise.

The commander tells all of us to be seated and we do as such. At this point we are all pretty confused but it's dead silent I'm looking around and I see two females standing in the back almost crying. They are instructed to report to the base commander and March to the desk in front of all us. They report in to him then with a very calm but stern tone the base commander said" You are being found guilty of article 92 how do you plea?" Both of the females respond at this point sobbing "guilty sir". The Colonel went on how drinking underage, being in a male's room, and having contraband is un acceptable and a disgrace to the Marine Corps. He further went into detail about the Males involved in this incident will be incarcerated for the remainder of their enlistment but doesn't not excuse their actions. He ask them if the have anything to say at this point hysterically crying they say" no sir". Finally I realized I was witnessing my first Public NJP (Non-Judicial Punishment is how the military punishes you without taking you to court). He tells them they are being reduced to E-1 will be confined to the barracks with no electronics for 60 days and will being receiving half pay for the duration of the confinement. He then commands them to dismiss they turn around and march off with a trail of tears behind them. It was crazy seeing that but it definitely set the tone for the rest of my time at the school house learning my job.

If you haven't noticed while Camp Johnson is where "I learn my job" I haven't talked about it at all. The reason for that is because schools in the Marine Corps are complete fucking jokes. I studied for about one test while there and for the rest used the process of elimination to answer all my test. I wasn't top of my class by any means but I got by just fine. During the day we spent a lot of time clicking through slides and hearing the instructors go on long lectures about things that we will never use in the fleet and they mentioned it quite frequently how useless the material is.

    There really is only two good parts from the school house I have worth sharing. The first is my time in Mr. Terrell's class. Our school had several instructors some Marines and some Civilians Mr. Terrell was a retired Marine he was about 1000 years old and was just one of those mean old black men that hated on us a lot because he was in Vietnam and we was boots. The issue with his classes was they were so god damn boring. Talking about how diagrams that show how wires can run is boring material to begin with but he managed to make it drag out for eternity. I frequently fell asleep in his class.

There I was in class sitting next to Bruce.

He was on a mission to have the best grade in class and was kind of a teacher's pet. Still loved him but sitting next to me he got his revenge for me fucking with him outside of school. He would pinch me, push my hand out from my face, and whatever else he could think of to wake me up. I was sitting there trying to sleep in class Bruce was being extra douche today waking me up and Mr. Terrell caught me. What happened next was him turning up his crazy old black man level over 9000. He looks at me takes off his glasses and just holds his hand up. He starts walking closer to the point where I could smell he drank black coffee. He shows me his hand and spits all over it with richoet getting on my uniform. He then goes "Boy if I catch you nodding off one more time, I'm take this hand and slap you so hard my DNA is going to become a part of you. Then one day down the road you're going to have kids and those little bastards are daggon look just like me. Do you want that boy?" I woke the fuck up disgusted, scared, and completely creeped out I tell him "no sir". At that point I didn't sleep at least in Mr. Terrell class anymore.

While in our school we are supposed to learn how to fix trucks the only time I actually got dirty and was turning a wrench was in the section where we learned how to pull engines. At this point I have never done that much mechanical work the most being changing oil and a flat tire. Pulling an engine is one of the manliest feelings you ever will have.

By the time you get to section of school where I was going to pull an engine I have been there for about two out of the three months. We have spent hundreds of hours clicking through power point style presentations and maybe a few hours actually touching a truck. Safe to say we was all excited to be out of the class room and going to be on our feet being active for the week.

The building where they teach us how to replace motors was on the opposite side of the lot that housed all of our classrooms. It was pretty large building it had about 12 bays which are about the size of one car garages. Our class marched over there and put on coveralls for the first time. As we get our coveralls put on we start getting grouped up into our groups. Just like any school group you have your typical set up the guy who does all the work aka me, the guy who hides till the end his name was yap, the guy lost in the sauce, and then the guy who tries to help but is a lost cause. Our group definitely seemed like the rejects considering I was the best guy and my mechanical skills didn't exceed much past changing oil.

Just like most things that are complex there is instructions how to do it we call these books, Technical Manuals or TM's for short. I'm reading the instructions figuring out where to start and the first step is removing the radiator. First thing I do is put nothing to catch any fluids on the ground I take off the main hose to the radiator and all the coolant comes out like a fire house going everywhere. It's a huge mess and I start freaking out luckily one of the instructors was close by and he threw a huge drip pan perfectly to where it caught all the coolant. Covered in coolant and embarrassed that is how my first task as a mechanic begins.

I'm moving along finally got most of the parts the requiring fluids removed and they were all over the floor. I learn about the magic of dry sweep. Dry sweep is basically dirt you put over oils and hazardous fluids and rub it around so it soaks it all up. The way we learn how to rub the dry sweep into the ground effectively was by putting the song stanky leg on. This was like the number one song at the time and made cleaning up our mess a lot of fun. At the end of the day the instructors put on two songs over the shops audio system first was stanky leg. After our whole class was done dancing over dirt our next song was Clean up by Barney and the gang. For some reason the instructors at motor removal section got a kick out of that song and played it every time. My first day actually working on a truck my nails were black, my hands scratched up, and my whole body felt drenched in oil. I loved every second of it.

As the week went on we got closer and closer to pulling out the engine. It doesn't take multiple days to pull a motor but when you got 4 idiots doing it step by step from the book it's a process. The moment finally did come we had the motor attached to the engine lift and after finessing it for about sure enough it was out. We sat there staring at it and I had quite the sense of pride come over me that moment was great. The next part that comes though is the come down from the high. For everything you pull out you have to put back in. Pulling stuff out is fun it's literally a matter of taking bolts or clamps off and pulling that's it. But putting things back on is where it gets tricky you have adjust things, align holes, torque bolts, tighten nuts, and overall just a lot more attention to detail then removing components. Where it took us about a day and a half to pull the engine it took about three days to put it all back together successfully. After that long process is complete there is another sense of pride that comes with installing a major component like that successfully and seeing it startup it feels great.

As our graduation date is only a few weeks away the Marine Corps drafts up all of our orders and starts getting our flights arranged. I will never forget this moment we marched back to the barracks from school one day. The class leaders was talking to one of the head instructors and gets the plan for the next day. All of the class leaders come back and dismiss each class except ours he is with the instructor still and comes back with a list. I knew it was something good because Hernandez hardly ever smiled but he was grinning from ear to ear with this list. He walks up and said " so. if you guys want to leave right now you can but I have the list where all of our duty stations are" He kind if plays it out a bit for dramatic effect but gets to it after a while. I hear him start at the top of the list and starts naming our names and where our duty station is. "Anderson 2/5 camp Pendleton. Alvarez 1st tanks 29 palms". Then came my name "Beach CLC 35 Kaneohe Bay, Hawaii". I lit up and squealed like a teenage girl. Getting Hawaii as your first duty station is like going to Vegas and hitting blackjack on the $1000 dollar tables. And surprisingly guess who was going with me Bruce and Tony. Loki got Lejeune and was pretty jealous of us.

We go back to our rooms Bruce and me are giddy as hell start researching all the hot spots and what to do there. Later that evening Loki comes back blacked out drunk with the attitude like he wants to fight. I haven't really described Loki physically but he was a bit plump he was about 5 foot 3 and not quite fat but definitely not that strong but he use to wrestle in high school so he was a little cocky for his size. He goes off and starts cursing at me and Bruce calling us bitches and he hates us. Bruce and me laugh it off and keep going back and forth with pictures and videos of our soon to be home for the next three years. Then Loki decided to cross the line. He looked at me and said, "You wanna know how I know you're a bitch? I literally fucked your girl and you didn't do shit about it". Now I get being drunk and mad so I just kind of rolled my eyes but what he said next was what did it. Bruce said, "Hey man that's not cool you really need to go to sleep". Loki replies with" Your just lucky you fiancé isn't her because I would have fucked her too!" At that point I have never really seen Bruce get upset and he wasn't big by any means either little bit smaller then me about 5 foot 8 and 160 pound or so.

But Bruce was from Tennessee and had been doing farm work his whole life so for his size he had man strength. He got up from his bed I'm standing there ready to break it up if Loki got the upper hand but I was going to let Bruce let his anger out a bit. He squares up with Loki and said" what the fuck did you just say bitch?" Loki replies with " you heard me". I watched Bruce throw two solid ass uppercuts right to his stomach and knocked the wind out of him. As Loki was bending over Bruce grabbed his neck with one hand pushed him forward and moved him from the center of them room to where out closets were. Our closets we had were about a foot and half deep and three feet wide. On the front they had a lock so no one could go in them when we wasn't there. Dan's locker just so happened to be open with lock and key hanging on the handle. I watched Bruce hurl him into the closet and slam the door closed with him in there and locked it. I'm sitting there jaw dropped I am completely speechless. I see Bruce red in the face walk right outside with the locker keys and disappeared.

A few more moments go by and Loki starts banging on the closest. He tries to break it open but these lockers are from the 60s there solid metal and durable as hell it doesn't even budge at all. I hear Loki screaming inside the locker and I look at the front door wide open. I kind of chuckled, I turned on my stereo not very loud but enough to drown out him screaming and banging on the locker, I close the blinds, and head outside to smoke some cigarettes. I ended up sitting out there for about an hour. The smoke pit is right downstairs from where my room is so I could see the door. I watch Bruce walking back with a bag of snacks in his hand and a big ol chew in his mouth. I run up to him and ask how he is and without skipping a beat replies "good man, is that prick still in the locker?" I tell him what I did and he laughed we head back up to our room and open the door. The music is still playing but he stopped screaming and banging on the locker. We sit down at our beds and try and figure out the best course of action. For all we knew he was in there making prison shanks ready to kill us. We go and knock on the closest he makes no noise. We looked at each other clueless what to do next. Bruce opens it using the door as a shield as it opens up. There he sat in the field position in the most pathetic helpless look I have seen on a man. Bruce and me are ready for him to try and fight us but he just got up and walked out the door. We knew he wasn't going to tell on us because granted my word didn't mean shit but Bruce up to this point has been the perfect Marine in the eyes of our superiors and would side with him over anyone.

    The next couple weeks leading up to gradation was really awkward. We both knew the type of person Loki was and he only came to the room to sleep and get ready in the morning. He probably needed some type of mental help or was on the path to having a serious drinking problem. Regardless I never really cared much to help him at that point. Bruce tried to make amends with him but he didn't want to be a man and own up to his mistakes. It was kind of disappointing due to everything we had been through. But there is certain people you need to immediately cut out of your life and Loki was one of them. I ended up adding him on Facebook years later but still haven't talked to him since that night.

Chapter 7-Visiting Home

The Day is here gradation from the school house. I officially have the job code of 3521 automotive maintenance technician. I have my whole life packed again into three bags got my plane tickets to go home and then off to Hawaii. At this point the only time I have been home was for boot camp leave where it's an awkward time adjusting to being treated normal. Leaving the school house I was ready to show my friends back home how the Marines party.

After we graduate we come back all our bags are piled up in the center hallway. We sort through it and start to go our separate ways. I link up with a couple guys heading to the airport so we can share the cab fee and take my final glance at Camp Johnson. There was a lot of Happy and sad moments there but I wouldn't change anything about them. But best believed I was ready to take my 20 days of leave and head off to Hawaii. I get to the airport get all my bags checked in decide to have a nice meal before my flight and watch a movie on my laptop. Boarding starts on my plane I hop on and fall asleep as I watch my movie the only one I had downloaded at the time was the Matrix.

I land in Fort Myers airport and my father is right outside the security gate to pick me up. Coming home is always nice in the military seeing your family after being away for a while makes you appreciate the time you have with them and not get annoyed of them. One thing you do though is plan your visits when coming home. You make sure everyday you have something planned. I made sure to have girls hit up that are down to smash, my boys ready to turn up, and tickets to theme parks with my family in the works. As my Dad and me are walking out the airport I see his truck. I loved this damn truck it was such a beast it was a 2012 Ram 1500. This thing had all the bells and whistles it had the chrome bumpers it had 22 inch rims the thing was just the coolest thing ever to me and I wanted it so bad. He offered to sell it to me but my PFC pay couldn't put a dent into the payments of that thing.

When going home it's always the weirdest experience especially in you younger days in the military where the time in between going home isn't but a few months. The last few months you have had all of these life changing experiences meeting people from all around the country. But back home it stays the same for the most part. A road might get some construction done a gas station gets bought out by another one. But for the most part your friends, your family, and everything else is like you never left.

    I get home from the airport and greeted by my mom and our family dogs. I go and drop all my bags in my room. I come out and talk to them for a little bit we catch up and by that time its about 10pm. I tell everyone goodnight and head off to bed ready for my awesome plans to start happening. I wake up the next morning and decided I needed to try and stay in shape while home. I go out and run about 1 mile decide why the fuck am I doing this and walk home. My plans of working out while home was over I'm just going to smash and turn up the whole time. I come back home have breakfast. All my friends from high school are working there random jobs at chipotle or being a bum. I go hit them up and their smoking weed just like I never left for boot camp or anything. Here I did what a lot of people in the military do while on leave for more than a couple days, I smoked some weed. A lot of people don't admit to it but they do. I know at least a few dozen that did it anytime they take more than 15 days of leave. There's no way to stop it but the military doesn't like to mention it. Either way I knew my tolerance was going to be low so I only took a couple hits and was straight chilling. As I was sitting there with my friends Justin and Joseph told me there was a rave later that week and we should get some ecstasy and go there. We go online buy our tickets and Joseph gets the plug for the "ecstasy". We talk more about it and as I sober up I put my clear eye drops in, and head home. Back home driving on the influence while is completely retarded is super easy. Where I'm from every road is perfectly straight very open, wide lanes, and no pedestrian traffic. Almost like a drunk driver's heaven to navigate.

I get home to nice home cooked meal from my mom. At this point I have been an expert from hiding my drunk/High from my parents for years. I manage to eat my food and enjoy it without raising too much of an alarm. We all confirm our plans to go up to Orlando to go to bush gardens the next week. We talk about that and when my brother is coming home to visit from the navy in a couple days.

The first thing I wanted to do while home was get a tattoo. At this point every Marine I have seen that has been in for a while had one so I figured I needed one as well. The only problem was what should I get one of? Marine Corps stuff was just to cliché and basic. The guy at the tattoo shop told me he liked to get tattoos of stuff that made an impact in his life. At this point in my life the only thing that really made an impact in my life was strippers. Guess what 19 year old me decided to get a tattoo of? You guessed it a nice lovely stripper on my arm. I kind of wished it had more meaning but nope got a stripper right there on my right arm. I like to pretend it reminds me not to fuck with them anymore and it kind of did.

    The next part of my story is about Angela. She was my perfect body type D cup size tits, thick in the butt, nice legs, and wore glasses. We both go way back from middle school we always flirted around but really never dated each other. My final days of Johnson I had been doing what all Marines do prior to going home is putting in work for leave pussy. It usually starts about a month prior to going home you hit them up on Facebook. The typical routine is you ask them how there doing, and you really miss seeing a familiar face. 9 times out of 10 they eat that shit up. You keep playing that game of being far from home and just want someone to spend time with while back home. You feel alone because everyone you knew is gone or doing something else and has no time for you. Either way we schedule a date and I take her out to the classiest establishment I knew of Olive Garden. We eat our food the date is going perfectly. We wrap up our dinner and head to the movies I think we saw one of those exorcism movies. We start fooling around in the theater and I think to myself I got this shit in the bag after god knows how many years I'm finally going to beat cheeks. We head back to her house, no one is there I figure it's good and then for the first time I get blue balls. I walked her to the door she thanks me for the night and just runs inside and closes the door. I'm looking around confused as hell wondering what does my dick do now?

Well you know how Angela has been the girl I have been trying to get with on and off for the last 7 plus years. Everyone has to have their old reliable when they go home. You guaranteed laid at any time anyplace for me it was Jamie. She was a cute girl nice big butt not the best face but was good enough to fuck. I hit her up around midnight and just like clockwork she was down to fuck. The problem was I wanted more of a challenge in my life and having someone that would put out any time of the day while nice for my dick didn't give me a nut for my mind. But accepting defeat I let my dick do the thinking like most men and gave up on Angela and hopped on Jamie for the remainder of my time home. The best part she lived walking distance away from my parents' house.

The weekend comes and that rave I was talking about was about to happen tonight. My dad decided to be generous and let me use his truck that night so I could scoop up all my friends and pull up in style. I go by and scoop up all of my friends to include Justin and Joseph and we head up to where the rave is about a 45-minute drive.

We get there and I'm pretty sure it was one of those trampoline places. There was foam pits, ropes to climb, monkey bars, all of this was going on while people were tripping on drugs and listening to house music. About 10 minutes before we get there we all take our ecstasy pills. Before you get butt hurt we brought blankets and pillows to sleep in the truck I did not plan on driving on ecstasy. We get there and head in and there's a bunch of people we know there and we meet up and start dancing having a good time. About an hour goes by and I still feel nothing all my friends are high as shit and I'm sober as a judge. I take another one and another hour goes by still sober as hell. I'm walking around still having a good time but kind of bummed these drugs aren't working. I try everything to get it kick started pound a red bull have someone do the fingertip light show for me and nothing. After a while I'm just outside smoking cigarettes like a chimney when a guy I knew from high school walks up and we start chatting. I tell him how I dropped E and haven't felt shit after 3 hours he smiles and ask you want to do something that will work right now? I look at him slightly confused but agree and he leads me into the bathroom. He pulls out a debit card and his phone places them down on the back of the toilet bowl and then out came his bag of cocaine. I get a little nervous but fuck it I'm already in here can't be a bitch. He lines it all up and I take my first line of coke. The next feeling can only be described as HOLY SHIT! I never felt so hyped in my life everything became amazing and I had unlimited energy. We left the bathroom and I went out on a mission I wanted to fuck someone immediately. With my new fount energy and confidence it didn't take but about 10 minutes before I had some rave girl she was skinny had blond hair and the need for dick it seemed. Back in that same bathroom bent over the sink I start railing her out. I get done with her and I'm still hyped as hell and on one. I make my way to the trampolines and start jumping around trying to let some of this energy go, I start making conversations with strangers just being friendly with everyone. I felt like the hottest man on the planet. That feeling lasted about a solid 2 hours. Then the come down started to come. I sobered up really quick after the cocaine wore off and decided it was time to go home. I dropped everyone off and you would think I would have felt guilt for doing drugs but I didn't. The only thing I realized was that I couldn't do cocaine again because I knew I wouldn't ever be able to get the same high I did that night.

I decide to end my partying for the rest of my time while home mostly because I needed to ensure my piss was clean before going to Hawaii. I still had about 15 more days till I left so I wasn't really sweating the drugs at all.

As my days to leaving got closer and closer my parents started to get really sad. I felt bad for leaving them but I was going to Hawaii its not like you can be upset with a plane ticket that has Honolulu international airport on it. I spend my final days taking pictures and helping my dad work on his project car his 1965 Mustang. That car was a beast I'm still upset he sold it to this day. When he got it the dude rebuilt the motor and did all the mods to it the thing was fast as hell. My final day I said I was going to stop by my friends' houses and say bye to them all.

My dad throws me the keys to the mustang and told me "keep it under 100". I laughed and hugged him as I walked out the door. I hop into the Mustang and turn it on. The V8 on that thing always gave me the chills I can hear it as I write this. I pull out of the drive way and get about a mile away from my house. I pull on to Immokalee road and I look around not a soul insight. I drop it in first and as I turn floor that thing and it fishtails hard but the rear tires are so fat it catches it almost immediately. I see the gas gauge is at about a quarter and decide I should get some gas to replace all the fuel I'm about to burn. I pull up to the gas station down the street from my house and almost immediately get like 2 or 3 people comment on the car. At this point I knew how it felt to be a rich kid driving daddies car the only thing was my dad decided to be rich after I left the house so I didn't feel that spoiled. I fill up the tank and get back on the road when I look to my left and I see a "souped" up Honda civic with no hood.

    Where I grew up we had a lot of Cubans and a lot of them tries to be into the "tuner" scene. They drove all the Hondas you could imagine. The only thing was they were broke so their "mods" didn't really go much past an exhaust tip and a K&N air filter. There was even one who decided for "weight reduction" would take off his hood (it rains pretty much every month in southwest Florida).

Back to the story I see him and him and his friend looks at me and I shit you not with a straight face starts revving up his motor. I grin and lightly tap on the gas it completely drowns out his car. He literally redlines it in neutral for a solid 30 seconds. I think about giving him a head start just to make it a little fairer. Then remember fuck that cant disgrace American Muscle like that. The light turns green I drop it and it wasn't a huge wheelie but the front end came up off the ground and my ass could barely see the road ahead of me. I shift into second and the hood goes down I can see clearly again. I'm already about 100 yards through the intersection as I shift into third look back this dude just barely got through the intersection. I don't know how much I beat him by but I actually did listen to my dad and stopped at around 90. Then he did the most ricer thing he could do. As you can see from my brake lights I have slowed down where most people usually line up race again or give kudos to the car that just beat them. These guys pass me doing about 120 and I decided why not flex one more time. I drop it back into second and as the car forces me in my seat I catch back up to him in mere seconds I pass him again laughing my ass off at this dude trying so hard to flex on me. I make my turn and sadly never get to race him again.

I pull up to my friend Larry's parents' house because that's where usually where all my friends went. It was kind of the place where they all smoked weed together. I go inside and there they all are. I tell them I'm heading out tomorrow and say my goodbyes. I make a joke on my way out to stay right there and I'll see them when I get back. It completely goes over there head, I kind of chuckle to myself and leave.

I head back home and give my dad the keys. He looks at me for a second and goes "you know I think I heard some tires squealing earlier down the road a bit was that you? "I grin and reply "I couldn't that car is so slow it couldn't beat a bicycle in a race". We laughed for a bit, I got my whole life now packed up into 4 bags, we sit around the living room and I enjoyed each other's company my last night home. My dad asked me whens the next time I would be home and I made a promise "I will be home for Christmas".

Chapter 8-MCBH Kaneohe Bay, HI

The fleet at this point in your military career is all you have been talking about for awhile at this point. You have heard horror stories of being hazed, crazy barracks parties, working, being with real Marines, going on field ops, and going on "deployments". It's like a mythical place of amazing opportunities that you haven't been to yet. The fleet to give a simple answer is where we go to do our job. It's where you spend the majority of your time in the military. For me the fleet was aboard Marine Corps Base Hawaii Kaneohe bay, Hawaii. When I landed in Honolulu airport I met up promptly with Bruce, Tony, and this dude I barely knew his name was Steven we went to the USO which is the place in airports where military can go relax and get some snacks. Usually when you hit the fleet you have a point of contact and they arrange to come get you from the airport. We did not. Our orders said Combat logistic company 35 the guy who worked at the uso who knew what units were on K bay looked confused and thought maybe they messed it up with CLB-3. He gave the ood a call (officer of the day) which the guy in charge of the unit after normal working hours. He told the guy he would be there soon. We wait patiently for what felt like hours.

The van pulls up and he instructs us where to put our bags in the van and we take off. It was at night but even so the views was all nothing short of incredible. We get to the unit headquarters and walk over to the OOD office he goes through all of our paper work and set us up with our barracks room. Tony and me are in one room then Bruce and Steven are in another room. The OOD takes us over to the barracks and just like in all the movies I see all these guys hanging outside drinking beer staring at us. We lug all of our stuff up to the third floor and go to our rooms. I was expecting a little bit more but it was just like the barracks rooms at camp Johnson but newer stuff. All the furniture was made of wood looked a lot nicer then camp Johnson but not by a lot. I was happy as hell though I was in my new home. When we checked in was a Friday so we didn't have to worry about checking in officially till Monday. Tony and me decide to head down to the smoke pit and that is where I met my first friends in the fleet.

There was a guy named Devin he was your smoke pit guitar player. Then there was Dianna she was like the momma bear and gave advice to everyone. They can tell we are obviously new and start talking to us about everything what's our jobs are, where we are from, and what there is to do here. I was expecting to get fucked with immediately. Somehow after Devin and Dianna are showing us around we get one of those pocket-sized bottles of booze given to us. Tony and I go back to our room and polish all of it.

Hammered as hell we head back down to the smoke pit. This time though there some different guys there one is this Mexican looking dude with a big head and a white guy that kind of looked like a wanna be Eminem. They look at us and we don't say anything to them. Then they get really close and start yelling at us "What so we don't get a greeting or any shit like that?" They are wearing regular clothes so there is no way we could possibly identify what rank they are. We stutter "uh good evening gentleman". Then they proceed to ask us if we have been drinking at this point they are straight up bullying us. Tony and I could have definitely kicked their Asses but we have now been in the fleet for about 4 hours and are trying not to get in trouble day one. We get them to back off and I realize I'm dizzy drunk and decide its best if we just go back to our room. I don't remember much because I was passed out but from what Tony told me they was trying to come into our room and he pretty much pulled a Gandalf and wouldn't let them pass.

We wake up the next morning and since we had no car decided to just walk around the base. I have never seen anything like it from walking out the barracks to going by the gas station everywhere had amazing views. After we got back from walking around the base for a few hours we headed back to the barracks. When we got back the Company Gunnery Sergeant who is in charge of pretty much the administrative stuff and making sure new people get checked in. The Guy name was Gunnery Sergeant Kennedy he was a small white guy with full sleeves. He's to this day is my text book definition of a Gunny. At work he would always have a coffee mug in hand most likely with booze in it and just walked around talking to people all day. He was cool as the other side of the pillow. He got all our info and put us in contact with one of the Lance Corporals who's been there for a bit to walk us around on Monday. After that quick 30 minute conversation he told us to have a fun weekend and be ready for Monday. We didn't really do much but make sure our uniforms were good for Monday.

Sunday evening comes around and Lance Corporal Smith comes by and checks our uniform and everything seemed good.

He told us he would come get us in the morning and have us check in. Monday morning we wake up and get our uniform on and walk through the motor pool. Everyone is looking at us in our uniform because it's like the equivalent to a business suit but way more uncomfortable, on top of it being 85 degrees outside lets just say we look ridiculous. I see all the trucks and scoping out everything from the front gate to the office we are headed into. We get in and march in front of the company first sergeant who was First Sergeant Molina. He critiques our uniform and pretty much roast us for a bit. He then tells us where we are going to be working is in the Motor Transport Maintenance platoon aka MTM. He has Gunny Kennedy take us over and introduces us to the Marine in charge of the platoon her name was Gunnery Sergeant Matthews. We introduce ourselves and she has her Shop Chief show us around this guy name was Sergeant Ballarmstrong but we just called him Sergeant Ball. He shows us the restrooms, changing room, tool room, and the bays were we work.

There is about 20 plus Marines we see but didn't remember hardly any of them names. He tells us this is where we are going to be working after we get all our check in stuff completed. We go back to where the 1st sergeant office is and meet up with Smith. He takes us to his jeep and starts taking us around base completing all our check in stuff. It takes about the whole week to get our medical, dental records, and all our info turned in. The last step is getting CIF which is all of our gear we use like flack jackets, Kevlar's, packs, and so on. It's about 5 grand worth of gear and this is where your first major mistake in the fleet begins. Being young and dumb I didn't check my paperwork and they claimed to issue me "3 removable belts" let's just say that ended up biting me in the ass a few years down the road.

One thing a lot of people forget to mention when being stationed overseas or a place where cost of living is really high you get this thing called COLA. I have no idea what cola stands for but it boosted my lousy E-2 pay from 500 bucks a pay check to over 800 a paycheck. The second week in Hawaii I got paid that plus all my traveling fees the military gives you after you fly it supposed to compensate hotels, food, and etc. but I never needed that much money when travelling because I'm not retarded and know how to use the dollar menu. It was about 2 grand and I felt like a straight baller. What did I do next was kind of a boot move but luckily my father via internet and phone walked me through the process of buying a car. I went on my second weekend in the fleet and got a 2010 Mercedes Benz C300. It was nice as hell I really loved that car. With that I was able to start exploring the island with Bruce and Tony. We go see all the sights Pearl Harbor, Waikiki Beach, North Shore and all of it being amazing.

Monday comes around and someone told Sgt Ball I bought a car. You would think its not that big of a deal its your money spend it how you want. Just to give you the basis during my whole time buying this car my dad was on the phone with me had already checked the car fax, looked at all the pictures on the dealership website and talked to the salesman before I got there. I get in there and sit down and look at all the paperwork it all looks good. I walk out the door paying a total of 12 grand for the car, had interest rate of 4 percent, and my payments were about 180 a month. Not bad at all for your first car you bought on your own at 19. The only problem was these guys aren't use to 18-19 year olds getting good deals on cars. What your typical Marine gets is about a 15-year-old V6 mustang for almost double the value with an interest rate of 20 plus percent and a monthly payment of about their whole paycheck.

After I explained my details to Sgt Ball he was like "oh that usually doesn't happen, uhm well go get with the corporals see what the plan is for the day". I walk off and head down to where the Corporal office is. At the Desk there is Corporal Diego. Corporals are pretty much like leads in the regular world they work just like everyone else when needed to but if there isn't much going on they're for the most part chilling. He looks at me and said "go to the tool room, get a tool box". I comply and walk over and that is where I meet Corporal Benedict. I don't know how to describe him but he was a complete douche. This guy spent his whole day playing on his phone stuttered an aggravating amount and just really pissed me off. I don't know what it is but everyone in tool rooms are annoying as hell. After this dude takes ten minutes to just say I'm dumb for buying a car, he shows me my toolbox and an inventory sheet. I go through it all making sure everything is there and sign it. After I finish that I go to head back to Cpl Diego then this bitch stops me. He proceeds to stutter for another 5 minutes and tells me I need to inventory all of these special tool kits for him. Being a PFC and him a CPL I don't really have any choice so I start doing that. Time goes by and its time for lunch. We break for lunch at 1130 and come back at 1.

I meet up with Bruce and Tony and there telling me about all these cool trucks there working and I get a little jealous. I inform them of the amazing inventories I've been doing all morning and they laugh.

Later that week Tony and me are walking home and stop at the smoke pit. We see the same two guys who was messing with us our first night. We walk up and we see their rank. They are fucking lance corporals and not salty ones either. While lance corporal is a higher rank then me. Bruce got promoted from being first in class and Tony had a decent recruiter so they were both already Lances so it wasn't a real authority figure rank. Tony and me being a lot ballsier now call them out. They laugh at us and sit down right next to us and start talking to us. The Mexican dude name was Trejo and white guy name was Parish. They tell us how they were drunk and were sorry and to make it up to us they had extra tickets to a NAS concert the following weekend. We shake hands and make up, pretty excited to be going to a NAS concert.

The Friday finally comes where we go to the Nas concert. Parish and Trejo come over to our room and we start drinking. I was the only one with a car and Tony agreed to DD. We start turning up at the barracks getting our pre game on then around 8pm we head out. As Tony gets on the highway Trejo tells him there is a back way with way less traffic. At this point I have only seen the pretty parts of highway and while most of it is amazing there is some nasty ass spots in downtown Honolulu. We turn on to this street and I see all the shopping Carts and trash you could imagine. Up until this point Hawaii has been a magical oasis but when you have a city with couple million people there is going to be a ghetto. We get to the venue and head into the concert. I get in there and a couple of the warm up guys are still going through there sets.

We are dancing having a good time. I get grinded on by this big booty black chick and I love it. I then made a pretty big mistake. I touched this woman hair and she flipped the switch on me like I killed her first born over all the music she screamed " why the fuck you gots be touching ma hur" I replied to her "I'm sorry my bad" then she proceeded to go " I just don't get why you gotta be all up on me like that" and honestly confused but a little annoyed I go " so its okay I grind my dick all over you ass but the second I touch your horse hair that to far?" she obviously didn't like that and we went out separate ways for the rest of the night it was just Tony, Trejo, Parish, and myself hanging out having a good time.

Considering Tony, Meyer, and technically Bruce was single at this time there was a program for us called the single Marine and sailor program. This program for our unit was lead by this navy guy named Ryan Scott he was a little bit older then us and would end up becoming one of my best friends. I run into him one day and start asking him about all the events. He ask if I like country music and I tell him I listen to it occasionally. Ryan tells me about this event coming up where Toby Keith is coming to our base and performing. At the time I knew who he was but not how big of a deal he really is. I start brushing up on his music so I know some more of his songs.

The day comes and we all get dressed up in flannels looking country as hell and ride over where the concert is going to be. This place is packed I did not expect the turnout it got but it had to be every single military member on the island. Since all of us were under 21 and every single Marine we work for is there it would be best to not drink at all.

The way it was set up was toward the back of the field it was area for people to sit with there kids and close to the food stands. After a certain while there was one of those barricade fences separating the sitting area from the standing area. I decided I wanted to go all the way close to the stage as possible. Everyone else in my group decided to stay in the sitting area. I make my way slowly up to the front and like clockwork get there right before Toby Keith comes on stage.

He comes out and is doing great not missing a single beat. If you ever been to a Toby Keith concert you know he takes beer breaks after a few songs. He is looking through the crowd saying hi to people and the works. He looks at me and I shit you not ask me "Hey son where's your beer?" I reply "I can't drink sir". After that I watch him walk over to his cooler and open it up comes back with a bud light and goes "Son you can drink today". I caught it and it made my night. I just received a beer from Toby Keith who is going to give me shit for underage drinking? I stand up front for a few more songs and I head back. Bruce and Tony didn't believe me but I didn't care. I tried keeping that beer can but lost it not even a week later.
The next few months was more or less becoming a big family with my platoon. Being on an island where it cost at least $1000

just to go home you learn to depend on each other. Cpl Diego became our big brother in a sense he really looked out for us in our early days and taught me a lot. One thing that I owe to him is he taught me how the Marine Corps will pay for you vehicle to be shipped out to Hawaii. Armed with that knowledge I had a pretty big plan for next time I went home. As time goes by you start to make a list of things to do in Hawaii and promptly knock them off one by one skydiving, every hiking trail, surfing, deep sea fishing, north shore, camping, luau's. It's a pretty big list of things to do but when you're living there you knock it out in about 6 months. I feel pretty content work is going good but I was missing something. I haven't got laid since I came out to Hawaii and boy was I desperate!

The next part of my story is about Luna. One of the guys I was friends with was a bit of a man whore and tried to fuck everything he introduced to me POF which is called plenty of fish. Prior to using Tinder where it's straight and to the point you actually had to look for these girls and talk to them and even go on dates. At first I make fun of him and say I'm never going to use the Internet just to get laid. Soo a few hours later sitting in my room I have downloaded POF and made a profile. I start messaging every single girl on the app I can.

I get a few responses but they were just way to busted. I finally get a response back from one and she didn't seem that bad it was Luna. We start talking and everything is going great we set up a date and once again I'm going to one of the most premier establishments the Cheesecake Factory. I go by and pick her up. Cat fishing wasn't really a phrase back then but lets just say her pictures were definitely old and using the angles to the max. She was a big ol girl weighed at least 200 pounds and I was pretty disappointed. I thought about just kicking her out of my car and going home. But I'm a pussy and this poor girl probably hasn't had a guy take her out since 30 pounds ago. I load her up in the Benz strap her up and head over to the other side of the island. One thing I will give big girls is they have personalities; she was funny and could make for good conversations. I start to get over how she played me and start to enjoy myself. We get to the factory of cheesecake and get seated. She tells me how she was born and raised here but wanted to leave. I listened to this girl's life story, thinking I better get a great blowjob from this. The night goes on and as we are leaving she basically pulls the dip and said she had to pick up her friend down the street. Pretty sure she was lying but whatever I had a good meal and headed home.

She text me the next day apologizing for leaving and wanted to make it up to me. She said she had a bottle of patron and wanted to go sit on the beach and finish it with me. At night most beaches have some type of patrol making sure hobos don't get washed away or something. There is one exception though the beach on base. At night time it is completely dead. You have to drive across the airstrip and it's not a beach you can just accidently walk up on. I go and pick up the whale and this time she a lot touchier with me; I just want the tequila so I let it ride. We get to the beach and I had one towel in the trunk of my car we bring it down and go sit in the sand with the moon lighting the ocean it was actually quite romantic. We start taking swigs of it and about 30 minutes in we are drunk. We start making out at this point and she goes down on me and proceeds to give me the greatest blowjob on the planet. Even with whiskey dick she makes me nut in record time. I look up at the sky feeling so relaxed I pass out almost immediately.

A few hours go by and she wakes me up. Groggy as hell we decide to bury the bottle. I always wondered if it is still buried on that beach. We head back to my car and go back to sleep for a few more hours. I wake up again and the sun just barely rising I decide to take her home. As I'm pulling out from the beach parking lot I get pulled over by the military police. I'm scared as hell not sure if I still have alcohol on my breath. The limit for an underage Marine on base is 0.00 so if I have to blow I'm done for DUI on base.

The MP comes up to the car and sees me with the whale and I don't know if he just had pity for me or what but he gave me a look of disappointment and tells me to get her home safe. I take her home and head back to the barracks.

You ever hear that old saying Fat chicks are like mopeds its fun to ride but no one wants to be caught on one. Well that couldn't be a more true statement I completely avoided introducing her to my friends. I wanted to cut her off but those damn blowjobs were so good. She was a freak and wanted to do it everywhere. On the beach, in the movies, in the park, at the mall, hell she even sucked my dick going through the drive thru of a Wendy's. Let's just say the guy at the cash register would never forget that day.

I keep on wanting to break it off but when you're getting the best head on almost a daily basis your dick over throws your mind. But thankfully it had come to an end.

When doing your yearly rifle qualification on Hawaii the range is on the complete opposite side of the base. What does that mean? Your waking up at about 4 am every morning to be there and ready to shoot by 7 am. We usually wrapped up around 3pm and make it just in time for Hawaii traffic. The traffic in Hawaii has been rated the worst traffic in the country and it earns the title daily. We are lucky to be back by 6pm at the end of the day. During this time Luna has been blowing me up a ridiculous amount even after I tell her I'm going to be busy this week. Tony and me decide to grab some burger king right off base when we got back one day. We go there and somehow this stalking bitch harassing me that I went there and didn't come see her. What I did next was what they call now a days ghosting. I blocked her on everything and never talked to her again after that day. I had knocked out banging a fat chick off my bucket list and never wanted to repeat that.

At this point I was pretty content, everyone I worked with was cool. I knew my place and we was in a pretty productive section that was until Sergeant William Johnson checked in. My relationship with Sgt Johnson was a roller coaster I would despise him one day and the next day he's like a father figure. Sgt Johnson was intimidating from first impression to say the least he was about 6 foot 4 and weighed 260 pounds and looked like he could be a lineman in the NFL. At first he didn't really want to talk to Tony or me at all.

The only person he talked to was Bruce and that was because he was a few months from getting promoted so in retrospect he was trying to teach him how to lead his peers but we took it as he didn't like us. For at work he was designated as the guy who checks the trucks over before they leave but he had his assistant, Thor do all of the work so we rarely saw him even at work. A few weeks after he arrived someone told him to be more outgoing I think because he started coming out and talking to us. It was kind of annoying at first because it was just him bragging about how great he was. But considering we were Lcpls and he was a Sergeant we smiled and waved. Then one day we kind of got into a bit of an argument. I don't remember the details but it was along the lines of when I thought I would be getting promoted and he flexed on how he decides when that will happen. I disagreed and said as long as I keep doing what I do I should be good but that really pissed him off.
The next week he grabs a guy named Aaron and me tells us this isn't a punishment but we need to go to another unit and help them fix trucks.

We both knew that was bullshit but we comply and head over to a unit called 3/3. This unit is where the majority of the Marines are infantrymen and these guys are all salty Afghan and Iraq war vets so trashing trucks was basically there middle name. The trucks Aaron and me had to fix were so messed up it probably cost more to fix them then it would have been to just order a new truck.

But the Marine Corps didn't care and we had work. While being over there at 3/3 they had a lot of side things they had to do throughout the week like classes and weapons cleaning to just name a couple so when they weren't there we would usually come back to our own shop. One Friday they decided to do a aloha Friday. Aloha Friday is a thing practiced on the island where everyone leaves work really early on Friday sometimes early as 9 am. This Friday around 10am 3/3 decided to have a aloha Friday. At this point Aaron and me have been working there for about 3 weeks. We decided since 3/3 was off we shouldn't go back to our work and check to see if there off, we are good. We head back to the barracks and are relaxing for about an hour and I get a call from Bruce. I answer and he ask where am I at in a very bossy tone. I tell him the barracks and he replies "stand by outside Sgt Johnson office right now". I roll my eyes as I tell Aaron what just happened and we head over ready to get our Asses reamed.

Sgt Johnson office door was outside and at the time the sun was shining directly where they had us standing. We stand there for about 10 minutes just as my feet start to fall asleep he opens the door. We both walk in standing right in front of his desk by the door enough to where the sun is still blinding us. I try and move out of the way and Johnson growls "get back in front of me". We stood there for what felt like an hour straight getting yelled at how we are complete pieces of shit and should be in the brig. He explained how we are basically no better then a deserter. He ended with how our cross rifles were his. (The cross rifles are what distinguishes the rank insignia between a Lance Corporal and a Private first class). At this point I know some of what he said was bullshit but the way he expressed he was going to have us demoted I was pretty sure he was going to make it happen. Remember GySgt Kennedy? Well luckily for every hot head is a level head senior to put someone in check. I watched Sgt Johnson explain it to him and obviously milking it for way worse then what it was. At the end all I heard was him laugh and go "that's it? I literally did that a week ago". Lets just say Sgt Johnson got me back in other ways.

There I was 5pm on Friday on my hands and feet doing "bear crawls" with a screwdriver scraping weeds out from the cracks in the cement. I go to stand up so the blood will get out of my head and all I hear is Johnson yell, " I didn't say stand up!" I go back down and continue scraping weeds with Aaron. The lot where all of our unit trucks are stored is a solid 2 acres at least. I bare crawled that whole entire lot that night and then I learnt I either needed to get really buff so I could beat up Johnson or be his bitch. I started hitting the gym a lot.

I was on Duty for Thanksgiving. Duty if I haven't really explained duty earlier, it is basically when you ensure no one in the barracks gets into serious trouble and mitigate incidents. On thanksgiving we got 4 days off. What do Marines do when they get 4 days off? They binge drink, eat, and just cause trouble. It wasn't that bad being on duty all the senior leadership was bringing me food and everyone just got paid so they was out in town, the barracks was nice and quiet. One of the guys I work with comes down stairs frantically I ask him what is wrong? He is clearly drunk but what I got from him was Thor got a DUI and was at the police station out in town. He asks me who is sober in the barracks and I honestly tell him no one. Even though I worked with Thor he wasn't one of the guys I was really close with like Tony and Diego. But we was a family and I couldn't leave him there. I figure if I could be down and back in 30 minutes no one would notice. Leaving while on duty is a really big offence like back in the day people use to get executed for that.

We come out the gate onto the H3 and I'm pretty nervous and want to get back I am flying. Its 3am so no one is on the road and I maxed my Benz out at 140mph. We get to the police station and they head in and take what feel like forever. They finally come out and Thor sees me in my car as he hops in still drunk said "hey buddy thanks for the ride, damn place loved me didn't wanna see me go". I at this point figure someone already fount out I left my post. I am aggravated and haul ass back. I pull up to the barracks and it looks like no one noticed I was gone. I felt the biggest feeling of relief come over me. Thor looks around and said "well I'm fucked anyway might as well turn up wanna come Dathan?" I look at him in my uniform with duty belt on with an expression that he is stupid and he walks off. Friday of that week Thor gets busted down a rank and is an LCpl just like me.
Toward the end of the year the Marine Corps shuts down essentially. We have 4-day weekends almost every week from

thanksgiving till after New Year's. Since I promised by parents I would come home I started the process of putting in the request to go home. One of the most flawed systems is our leave system. Granted yes we accrue 30 days of paid time off a year they make it where it is such a process people hardly never use it till the end of there time to get out earlier. Beside the point, tickets from Hawaii to Florida average about $1200 dollars and waiting to the last minute they sky rocket close to 2 grand. Remember how I was on Sgt Johnson bad side? Well guess who is in charge of sending my leave up and getting it approved, my boy Johnson. He used that as leverage on me and kept threating me saying he wasn't going to send it up. The shitty rule we had was we couldn't buy plane tickets till our leave is approved. There it was 2 days before I was suppose to go on leave and Johnson calls me in to his office. Everyone else already had there leave approved weeks ago and was ready to go except me. He looks at me and tells me how I should be grateful he was allowing me to go home. At this point I don't even want to slightly upset him so I fill up his ego and pretty much say he is the greatest leader on the planet, straight ass kissing. He tells me I can go on leave and get out of here before he changes his mind. I go back to the barracks and get the first flight I can find.

$1800 dollars later I got a plane ticket to go home. I'm keeping my promise to my parents.

Chapter 9- Laie Point & 808

Going home this time is a lot more family orientated. At this point I'm pretty confident in my mechanical skills so I spent a lot of my time with my dad helping him with his Mustang. As we were working on it he tells me "Yea I'm getting rid of the truck and mustang I'm over the shitty gas mileage". I look at him puzzled and try and convince him to hold on to both of them. He shuts it down and tells me if I really want them he will sell them to me for exactly what he owed on them. The truck was 23,000 and the mustang about 12,000. I look into the process of having the Marine Corps ship your vehicle and at the time there was a rule about how old the vehicle can be for shipping. I end up picking the Truck I sat down with my father and we did all the math after I sold the Mercedes I would be paying about 400 bucks a month for the truck and I call my bank get approved ridiculously fast. 2 days before Christmas the check comes in the mail and my first check I ever wrote was to my dad for $23,000. I officially owned the Ram now. I went out immediately to the truck and took all my dads stuff out of it jokingly. He sits there laughing his ass off ask me for a ride to the dealership. I take him there where he picks up a little Toyota Tacoma I ask him why such a size downgrade and he reply's "you'll see when your filling that thing up". Rest of my time home was spent getting all my paper work situated and get a date where they come and ship the truck. I'm stoked heading back to Hawaii knowing my truck is coming.

I get back and inform everyone my truck is on the way. This is kind of where Sgt Johnson and I started to get along. He really liked the truck enough to where he wanted to buy it from me before it even got there. I tell him no but if I every think about it ill tell him first. The day finally comes and I get a phone call saying its here. I head down to the shipping yard in Honolulu there I see it in the lot. It didn't seem real at first but driving around windows down music up I felt like the coolest kid at school pulling up to the barracks in my truck.

For the first year I only had one roommate, which was Tony of course. For young Marines it was almost always three to a room. One day our number was called and we got our third roommate his name was Steve Rogers. Another Person that I would develop a bond with over the course of the next couple years. The day he came we hit it off pretty quick showing him around the base and taking him out to eat. One day he ask us to go to north shore which is where they portray the whole island in the entertainment industry. We load up my truck with a bunch of us and start heading up the scenic coast line. We make stops at the poke trucks and everywhere with a view.

We stop at this place called Laie Point cliffs. If you ever seen the movie forgetting Sarah Marshall it's that cliff Mila Kunis jumps off of. What they don't show you in the movie is that the water there is very rough and underneath the cliff is a cave from the water beating it up over the years. I line up and jump off the cliff and land in the water. I emerge and the water is a little rough but I was okay at swimming and I head toward the cave and figure I can crawl out from there. I didn't notice at the time but everyone else that jumped swam right towards a rope to pull themselves up. I manage to crawl into the cave and just as I sit up the water comes in. The saying about unstoppable forces and immovable objects couldn't better describe my situation. I tried grabbing onto cracks in the cave floor but the water was so powerful it moved me 10 feet down the cave before I even realized it. At this point I look around my heart is racing and have all the adrenaline pounding through my veins. I look around for something to grab on and there it came again the water. I get thrashed up and down the cave I fold up into the field position I knew if I would have been knocked unconscious I was dead. The waves beat me around the cave for what felt like a lifetime. It let off and I was toward the edge. I see blood everywhere and look out and see the sand on a beach about two miles out with nothing but rocks and debris all along the way and decide I'm going to have to swim. I go to stand up on the edge of the cave and just before I jump I see a hole in the rocks about 10 feet above me. At this point the water is coming and I have about 2 seconds to either jump and start swimming to the beach or try and lunge myself into that hole. I jump as hard as I can and manage to get my arms through the hole and pull my upper body away from the where the water is hitting. The water comes in and knocks my feet around but I'm pretty steady. I look through the hole and see all these broken beer bottles and trash everywhere. At this point I decide to say fuck it the infection and having glass in my body is better than dying. Just as I am about to crawl my way through this hole into the glass I see Steve and a few other guys running down to me. I have never felt so relieved to see someone then I did Steve that day. They help me through the hole and get me back to where the truck is. Still hopped up on adrenaline they see me still breathing hard and hand me a beer. That day there was not enough alcohol on the island to get me drunk and boy did I try. But at the end of the day I still owed Steve one for saving my life.

After that lesson I learnt that the Ocean is to not be fucked with I decided to enjoy sitting on the sand, watching the waves was more my cup of tea. A few weeks later after my near death experience we decided to head back up the coast line this time staying far away from cliffs. We get to the beach and get everything set up. Everyone decided they want to go swimming in the water except me. I stick back and enjoy my beer and views. Up in North part of Hawaii is very spacious and not as crowded. You can find your patch of beach and for the most part no one is really going to be around you much. There is some beach front houses there but they got trees and bushes to block out the nosey eyes. Its probably one of the more isolated parts of the island. I was sitting there and I see a woman start to walk toward me. At first I figure she is just passing but as she gets closer its clear she is headed my way. Then I take a double take and shit you not no top on at all. This woman was text book milf. I try and play it off like I don't even notice her lack of a top. As she walks up she ask me for a lighter. Being the smoker I was at the time I give her one and she lights up a cigarette. To this day I still kick myself in the ass over this. She starts talking to me and tells me she lives like 4 houses down from here and just wanted to lay in the sand today. She then tries to invite me over and being the completely retarded fuck I am tell her no I need to wait for my friends in the water. She gives me a look that can be described as are you fucking retarded? She rolls her eyes and then walks off. Not even 2 minutes later everyone comes out the water and ask me what that was all about. Knowing how bad I would get roasted by what I just, I did tell them she just wanted a lighter and left.

Remember Thor? The guy who got the DUI? Well since he got demoted and confined to the barracks he re-assessed his friends a bit and started hanging out with Tony and me a lot more. At first I just kind of felt bad for him but he ended up becoming one of my best friends while out there. But at the time Tony and I weren't 21 so even when he got off restriction the things he wanted to do weren't really options for us. Tony was about 6 months older then me and had a lot more patience to go out to bars. I decided to get a fake ID off the internet, and next thing you know I was back to my mischievous ways. The first time I used it was when Thor and another Guy named Burnam wanted to go to a strip club. I really didn't want to go but peer pressure was a son of a bitch. This strip club we went to though wasn't like Jacksonville strip clubs though it was a no shit classy gentleman's establishment called 808. This was the type of place where you drink champagne and wear suits to. We get there and as we come up to the bouncer. I'm nervous but think I did a good job hiding my anxiety because he let me in. We ended up getting a table on the second floor overlooking the dance floor.

Just to give you an idea of how boojie this place is they had the sparklers on the bottles. When they came and poured us our drinks I remember just leaning against the railing looking at everyone downstairs thinking I made it. We keep drinking throughout the night and these strippers were not regular strippers they were Vegas high-class strippers. They were doing hand stands making things clap I've never seen clap before. The tricks they did on the poles were athletic level movements. Towards then end being the sleaze ball I was ask if one of them wants to come home with me. It was not the type of establishment that condoned that one bit, I get rejected and we decide to grab some tall boys and shotgun them before we go home. It was a great night but a horrible morning. I wake up the next morning and do the worst hung over task you do after a long night of drinking which is log into you bank app. My eyes barely open I see my credit card balance it was like 200 bucks and go "hey that's not too bad". Then I had an idea to actually click on the account and see the charges. When I clicked on it I had to do a triple take. It was 3,000 damn dollars!! A little piece of me wanted to cry but I made the choice to put myself on restriction and not do a damn thing for the next couple months. I ask Thor how much he spent and he laughed and said "oh they took me for about 2 grand". After I talked to him how he was so cool about it he explained it like this.

Money especially in the military comes and goes. Somehow every day before payday your close to broke anyway. Granted saving money is something you should prioritize and make a effort to do your going to waste your money on dumb shit because your young and don't have a lot of necessary bills. Why not two or three times a year just go out and make some good memories. I ended up paying it off in like 3 months anyway he had a point. It's better to do something baller once in awhile then little dumb things that waste all your money every weekend.

While Thor and me were being poor we decided to start bettering ourselves and go to the gym. Every Marine Corps base has at least a couple gyms on it. Since we was both broke guess what we did every day for at least a couple hours. Thor was my first legit gym bro. The hardest part in finding a gym bro is someone who is about as strong as you and consistent. The difference between lifting weights solo and with your gym bro is exceptional. You never can really push yourself because that's how you end up with weight stuck on you and look ridiculous. But beside the point over the next few months we blew up like balloons. The best part was since Johnson was our main boss at the time and he was also a gym rat our work life's got much easier since we were all about it and he was a monster. We would spend most of our workday asking him about lifting advice. Time goes by and we started to incorporate running into our workout. As much as I hated running I actually started to get pretty decent at it. I realized that one day we were all running with Johnson leading and he took off toward the end it was just Thor, Tony, and I. At this point I looked back and saw everyone just completely gassed and though huh that is usually me dying on the side of the road. I still wished I would have stayed in that good of shape it was the best fitness test score I ever ran while Thor was my gym buddy I scored perfect on my pullups and crunches, and ran three miles in 20 minutes all legit not cheating scores as well.

The first wedding I ever attended was Bruce's. It was pretty small about 10 people but it was pretty beautiful. The location was at this lookout right off the likelike highway and had the mountains and ocean all in the back drop of it. I was so happy for Bruce because I never really seen such a successful relationship beside my parents and it gave me hope I wasn't a lost cause. After seeing his wedding it made me decide I was going to take a break from getting with crazy women for a bit. For his wedding since we was all arguing who were going to be his best man Tony, Sam, and I all signed in the little spot on this paper as his best man. I took a picture of myself that day and it has been my Facebook profile picture since.

Chapter 10- Khole, Kimberly, and Tinder

If you haven't noticed for the majority of the year I wasn't doing much in the woman department. I decided to not put the pussy on a pedestal for awhile with the exception of going to that strip club. For the most part I kept up with that for the majority of the year. That was until Khole checked in. Considering the majority of our company was men we were like hound dogs whenever a new woman came around. It was Monday morning and we see this girl in her service uniform on and just cant help but notice she had some huge tits. This uniform usually makes anyone look like a 12 year old boy but you could see her tits a mile away. My roommate Tony who was a pretty boy took interest in her.

Somehow he ends up talking to her and he's one of those guys that just knows how to put on the moves. He isn't just a savage he actually listens to them and genuinely cares about what they say. Fast forward a few weeks she is in our room on a Friday night drinking with us. Around this time of year it is prime hurricane weather. It was pouring outside and Khole mentions she likes to play soccer so we go door by door gathering up everyone in the barracks.

We all go down and start playing in the mud we are all slipping and falling everywhere. Not to sure if anyone actually scored but it was a great time and I don't even play soccer. As the time goes by Tony comes up to me and ask if he can have the room to himself tonight. I agree and watch Khole and him go up. When letting your friend have the room to yourself what is a fair amount of time 2, 3 hours? I go to my friend Michael's room and we drink for a while and I look and see it's been about 3 hours since they went into the room. I head back and open my door and they are fucking like rabbits. It looked like they just ran a couple marathons back to back. The whole room just reeked of nasty sex. Tony looked at me without missing a pump and said, "I got you tomorrow". I shake my head laughing as I close the door and decide I'm going to back to Michael's room for the night. I walk into his room and he gets me to spill the tea. I ended up sleeping on his floor that night.

I wake up in the morning and head back to my room. They are both in his bed and laughing as I come in. I ask them how there night was and the response was tiring. At this point I did have one crush on a female in the barracks but the only person who knew that was Tony. Khole looked at me and told me she was going to get me hooked up with Kimberly. Kimberly she was a cute Asian girl that was textbook white washed. She had the nicest body not the biggest tits but made up in every other single department. I really had a thing for her but never really went through with it. At this point we knew of each other but that was about it. What Khole informed me was she was roommates with her. Tony reassured me that he's got me. Where I was at I haven't been in a functional relationship since I've joined the Marines.

Khole started to put in the groundwork for me and I just kind of sat back and looked pretty. A few weeks go by and she finally comes with Khole to come drink in our room. Luckily Thor was home on leave so it was just the four of us. Tony started pouring up the drinks and I was making small talk with Kimberly. A few hours go by and we are all drunk as hell Tony and me go down to the smoke pit to smoke and the girl's stay in the room. We get down there and Tony tells me it's going good and I got this. We come back up to the room and its about to go down. It is the perfect time and I start making the moves on Kimberly and its going good. We turn off the lights and get ready to start beating cheeks. I hear Tony over in his bed going to pound down and I do the same. Now Kimberly wasn't the best fuck by any means what so ever. But when you been having a crush on someone for the last year and add alcohol to the mix makes it seems pretty good. When we got done I felt pretty good about myself. We cuddled for a little bit and was out like a light.

The next few weeks seemed close to perfect. I was getting pretty close to getting promoted and thought I was in a good relationship. Double dates with Tony and Khole became a thing. We went to restaurants, movies, beach, everything you can think of. After about the third week though it started to go down hill. She started talking to me less and less. I did some digging and got the scoop she was about to get with some other Marine in the barracks. At this point I'm pretty devastated. I actually opened up to her and felt like a goof ball.

It was Friday and I actually managed to get Kimberly over to drink with Tony, Khole, and me. I was trying to be nice. But she was being really distant. I decided we should start taking shots. I don't know how many we all took but we killed a whole handle of crown. It was mostly Tony and I but we were all drunk. We was playing a card game Khole and Tony decided it was time for bed. At this point we have a bit of a routine where we have sheets set up dividing the room when we had sex. I get in bed and Kimberly starts to kind of piss me off so I do the spiteful power fuck. The spiteful fuck is where you get your nut quick as possible and roll over. I achieved it and rolled over and went to sleep.

What felt like maybe 30 minutes I wake up and see her sleeping? I see her phone lit up and it was a text from that guy she was about to leave me for. At this point I'm beyond spiteful. I wake up Tony and he is still pretty drunk. He ask what I want to do try and get back at her. For some reason I have a light bulb go off in my head. I whisper the switch a roo. He looks at me said fuck it why not and we go into each other's bed. At first I didn't really plan on fucking Khole she was actually became a pretty good friend at this point. But as Tony started doing his thing and railing Kimberly it kind of woke her up. She starts grabbing my dick and I thought to myself well to make sure my boy doesn't get caught I'm going to have to distract her. I try and drag it out long as I can but eventually I end up in balls deep. I remember thinking to myself damn her pussy is way better then Kimberly's. I'm sitting there from what started as like a necessary evil turned up actually into a really damn good fuck. At the end though I really had to make it an effort not to try and smash again.

Surprisingly the next day I'm talking to Kimberly and she is essentially breaking up with me. I never really had been broke up with before. I did what most guys would do call her every name in the book and act like an asshole. Looking back it was really childish but I didn't care I was upset. I was really depressed for about a week. It was even more upsetting Khole thought it would cheer me up if she showed me her boobs. I looked at her and was even sadder because I knew I could never fuck her again. Then at the end of the week I discovered a new app it was called tinder.

The tinder chronicles are pretty wild.
My first experience with a girl on tinder was possibly my favorite. It was this 22 year old named Sarah. She wasn't the hottest by any means but she was a solid 7. As we get to talk she tells me she's in school and just wants a guy who just wants to fuck and nothing else. It worked out perfect she lived in Kaneohe. We go and meet up over some food at the mall. We get to talking she tells me she just got out of a 2 year relationship. I tell her about my 2 week relationship. We laugh a

bit and we go back to her studio. It was strictly to business. She goes on top and gets her orgasm. I go on top and get mine. We cleaned ourselves up and I went home. It was pretty perfect for what I needed at the time. It lasted about two months. The only reason why we had to break it off was because she had to move back to the mainland.

What I really loved about tinder especially when it first started was how honest the girls were. Back in the day everyone knew tinder was if you was trying to get laid. You obviously wanted to meet with them in a public place to ensure they weren't trying to abduct you. But it usually ended up back at the girls place or back seat of my truck.

Sarah told me about her moving situation from the get go so I never stopped swiping on tinder. The next girl I ended up meeting with was a little more complex her name was Sammy. While Sammy was pretty attractive she was 5 foot 6 weighed 120 pounds. Had the perfect ass and loved to get railed from behind. It took me a solid two dates to get her in bed. I really loved hitting that but she was about as dumb as a door knob. She liked to talk but I really didn't care to listen.

When I went to Sarah apartment she had a roommate. At this point I had never really seen a Tranny. I have heard of them but really never seen one in person. This was all before the transgender movement it was still very new to most people. I come over one night and there he opened the door. He was about my size but was wearing a dress and heals. I take a quick step back and say my bad I'm at the wrong house. I start to walk away and chatter box Sarah comes outside and grabs me. She's walking me into her room and I'm just speechless at this point. I have a really shocked look on my face. I sit down on her bed as she close the door. I calmly whisper, "What the hell is that?" At this time the acceptance of transgender really was a taboo subject. She goes on a rant explaining how he is really nice. I should go talk to him, blah blah blah. I figure hell why not lets see what these type of dudes are like since I never met one. We decided lets just chill at their place and have some drinks. A few more of her friends come over. We got music playing, beer pong set up, and there apartment was a little small but it was good enough. I was killing it that night on the beer pong my partner being the tranny. I was having a great time. The night starts to swindle down and everyone starts to leave. It was just Sarah, tranny, and me. We are sitting on the couch trying to watch TV but Sarah like usual wouldn't shut up. I go to stand up tell them I have to piss.

Sarah said she would meet me in the bedroom. I go in do my thing and come out. As I'm walking to Sarah room the tranny confronts me right in the hallway. He grabbed my balls and said I should come with him tonight! I freaked the fuck out. I was drunk at the time but once he said that I sobered up and could just see every Man detail about that guy. I shove the fuck out of him and start yelling at him. Sarah comes out saying its ok. I proceed to tell her it's not ok. She tries to convince me to just try it out and see how I like it. At this point I'm sober as judge and fuck this shit I'm out. I grab all my stuff hop in my truck and drove my happy ass back to base. I definitely would have blowed something if I got pulled over but a DUI is way better then getting fucked by a tranny. I got home deleted tinder and went to sleep. Tony and Thor asked me what I was doing coming in so late I told them nothing and went to sleep.

Chapter 11- 21 and Saturdays are for the boys

While I have been out using tinder to the max I neglected my boys in the barracks. Everyone gave me a lot of shit for never hanging out with them. I decided to turn a new leaf. Up until this point we was all underage and could never go to any clubs or bars for the most part. I had a fake id but I didn't really want to test it against a legit security guard.

Going out for my 21st birthday there was a small group Tony, Jake, and this navy dude named diodore he just landed a few hours before and seemed cool enough. Tony decided to drive down to Honolulu and they ask me where I want to go and I tell them moose's. We find parking and throw away our tall boys we have been pre-gaming with on the way over.

I turned 21 technically on a Sunday morning. I was in line at moose's at 11:45. I got to the front of the line and the bouncer said he was going to give me the few extra minutes so I could come in. We go in and I had heard a lot about Moses from everyone who had been. It's set up kind of like a dive bar/ Club upstairs and a restraint downstairs. It is one of the best places to go in Hawaii if your trying to not get dressed up fancy and have a good time. I go in and my first legal drink at a bar was an AMF (adios motherfucker contains like 5 shots of liquor, some sprite, and some blue cocktail mix) courtesy of my best friend Tony. I start drinking and trying to pace myself a bit so I don't get blacked out drunk to fast. The guys I was with wasn't about it. Every few minutes I was dragged off the dance floor and fed a shot. They even got complete strangers in on it. About two hours go by and I'm so ready for the lights to come on and leave the bar and go home. While I knew about moose's I did not know about Kelly O'Neil's which was right across the street and was one of two bars in Honolulu with a last call of 4 am. I manage to rally myself together and after grabbing a hotdog walk over with the rest of people still wanting to party from Moose's. I get in and at this point I'm barely coherent. All I remember next was getting kicked out and running through the streets. We stole some construction cones and wore them like hats. At this point it had to be either really late or super early. We end up at a hotel bar and Tony orders us all a round of AMFs again. I drank about half of it before I woke up in my bed. I have drank a lot obviously over last couple years in the Marines but that was the first time I legitimately blacked out. I go and check on everyone that went out with me and when I went into diodore room it smelt like piss. Turns out when he got back to the barracks he pissed all over his suit case and all of his clothes just reeked. It was funny as hell. We all ended up going to Denny's and tried and pieced together as much of that night as possible.

Now being 21 drinking had a whole new meaning. Going out to the bars was my newest and time consuming hobby. One of my main weekly events was Wing Night aka single wife night aka Thirsty Thursday. Aboard MCBH they have restaurant for all ranks the Sgts and below had kahunas. The officers had their fancy beachfront restaurant. The senior enlisted had the rocker club. For me it was perfect walking distance from my room. Every Single Thursday no matter how late we get off work or had some crazy PT session the next day we went. It was a really bonding thing for our platoon. When this tradition first started we had just merged with another company so we all kind if disliked each other at first. But Thursday at kahunas brought us all close as hell. It was there I became friends with Ernest. He was the guy in charge of the mechanic shop merging with us and he really butted heads with Johnson. At the time I was loyal to

Johnson so I thought he was a douche and jealous. Until we bonded over Lynard Skynard.

It was our third of fourth wing night and they brought out the karaoke machine. I decide to break the awkwardness with Ernest and offer him a back scratcher (a super drink with a lot of booze and a back scratcher in it). We would all come in and say "Back Scratcher!!" in a really loud European accent and race to drink it. These drinks were fucking huge like a solid liter sized drinks. We all took our turns being the winner. Anyways after drinking one of those you're felling some type of way. I go over and start talking to Ernest I discover he's not a doucher and a really cool guy. We hug it out and bros being bros became homies from there on out.

The next day were always comical to say the least. All of us went to Kahunas except our top ranking people in our platoon and Johnson. Fridays every single one of us came in and had our own game plan to sleep it off. I would go to the very end of the lot where no one is and turn on a truck with A/C and locks. Climb up in it and use the combat locks and sleep till lunch. The guys with offices just locked their doors and slept. Everyone else had their own game plans that worked efficiently because I never knew where they hid.

The funniest part was Johnson coming to look for us. He was close to getting promoted so he became an asshole again and tried to threaten all of us. Luckily he was only close to and not promoted since a bunch of the guys was his rank he got told to fuck off a lot. He got really spiteful after a while and swore to make all of our lives a living hell.

He almost caught me once though. One Friday I was in my spot and for some reason I sat up. I see Johnson walking over. In armored trucks the windows are so thick and the truck is so high up you can't really see inside from the outside. He is really far but is staring specifically at the truck I'm in. I turn it off and slouch in the chair. I check the locks and ensure that both doors are locked. I peak up and he is still coming straight ahead like a freight train. It started to get really hot inside the cab and I'm trying to conjure up a plan. I figure if when tries to open one door I climb out the other he would never notice me. The doors are a few hundred pounds and loud as hell when they open. That plan probably won't work. He gets 10 feet from the truck. I'm mentally and physically sweating bullets. He comes up and looks at the hood. My heart is beating super hard. He writes down a number and walks away. I feel like I just pissed myself. I wait another couple minutes and get out of the truck. It feels amazing to have the wind hit my face. My whole uniform is covered in sweat. I walk back and see Johnson about 10 minutes later and he ask my why I'm so sweaty. I lie like a mother fucker and tell him some bullshit about moving barrels. He buys it and I ended up taking a nap on the toilet. That became my new Friday hangover nap spot.

Not every Thursday ended well though. One of our many wing nights we had a good ol bar fight. It was mostly our group that filled that place on Thursday but there was still other units that came to it. One particular Thursday the unit 2/3 just came back from there "deployment" to Okinawa and was trying to get blackout drunk. They are talking shit through most of the night. But it being on base you get fucked pretty much instantly for any incident involving alcohol. That night it was raining so when it was time to go and we was all standing outside underneath little awning at the entrance. We was all shoulder to shoulder with these guys who have been talking shit all night. Just like any group fight goes starts as a shove next thing you know we fighting. I was standing there trying not to get physical when one of these dudes pushed Ernest. I went over grabbed his shirt and went to throw him back. Just as I did that dudes buddy comes from behind puts me in a headlock and has me bent over. Without missing a beat the dude I just shoved hit me with an uppercut that cut open my face right above the eyebrow. Knowing I'm in a shitty situation I did a cheap shot. While bent over and right before I get hit again I cock back and whale this dude in the balls with everything I had. He starts to step back holding his junk. I then bite the guy holding me in the headlock and draw blood he lets go. Just as I'm about to back up and get ready for them attack he grabs my shirt and it was my favorite shirt at the time. It was a grey V neck that fit me perfectly. He ripped it off me and just before I go back to avenge my shirt we see the military police coming in hot. My buddies grab me up and we run off into the woodsy area right across the street. We are walking through this dark ass muddy area of base. I'm bleeding like a son of a bitch and use my favorite shirt now destroyed to soak up all my blood. That night wouldn't have sucked so badly if it wasn't for my shirt.

The next day comes and I have about an inch cut above my eye. I ask everyone what I should do and they all send me to see the corpsman. Navy Corpsman I love these guys but they aren't really the cream of the crop at medical practice. But considering my options were limited I went. Luckily for me is this thing called patient confidentiality and they couldn't ask me how it happened or anything about it. I told them anyway because I didn't know any better at the time.

I discovered later that day the top enlisted Marine of the whole battalion the Sergeant Major got the police report and was looking for who the culprits were. All he knew was someone that was part of the incident left bleeding a lot. He went to the medical and asked if anyone came in for something related to a cut. The Corpsman saved my ass that day. He harassed and yelled at them for about 2 hours trying to get them to give up a name. But they stood their ground told them it's confidential and wasn't going to tell them anything.

Later that day the Sergeant Major held a battalion formation. He had all of us which is about 300 plus Marines all standing in one area and by himself started to walk through and look at each Marine one by one. I tilt my hat as low as I can and wait. Having one person go through and interrogate 300 people is quite time consuming. We were there for about an hour and he made it through the first of four companies'. Then my saving grace came when the Battalion commander came out.

The battalion commander is pretty much the guy who is legit in charge of everything kind of like the CEO of a company. He comes out and tells the Sergeant Major it's over we don't have all day. They pull us all in give us a speech about how our behavior is unacceptable and will find us……….They never caught us.

Fridays after we got off work we went to a bar right by base called the shack. It was fairly close to base and had a really chill vibe. That same Friday it was Thor, Tony, and I decided to go. We had a DD already planned to get us so we was turning up. They had a killer happy hour on Fridays till 7pm for the price of a beer you get a shot for free. It was very dangerous special but we lived life dangerously. We are sitting at our table joking and having a good time. Guess who walks into the place? The dam Sergeant Major with a few of his buddies. We wave at him and he walks by said hello and then went and sat down. About an hour later he's drunk because happy hour at the shack can take down anyone and he gets us a round of beers and shots. He comes over tells us he appreciates what we do and that he is happy to be our Sergeant Major. We start smiling and thinks we are happy he is complimenting us. In reality we was holding back our laughter because literally 4 hours prior he said we was unacceptable.

Getting promoted in the Marines is always a big deal especially after Lance Corporal. When I was supposed to get promoted to Corporal I had an argument with the one and only Johnson. The argument was along the lines I didn't think just running a lot would make a Marine lose weight healthy and went on that a good diet is required. Johnson argued back running 5 miles a day would make anyone lose weight. I told him yes but it wouldn't be as easy to sustain without a diet. Either way I went back and forth with this dude literally said "I'm belligerent and didn't deserve to get promoted". I got upset and this is where I gave him the fuel to stop me from getting promoted I yelled "Your all talk! You said you was going to take my rank before and last time I checked I'm still wearing that shit!" I bought into what I said and held on to it till the first of the month when it was time to get promoted. The first sergeant comes down with all the papers with our promotion warrants on it and he told me "your not on the list beach". That feeling was pretty shitty not going to lie. I felt like Johnson played the biggest fuck you card ever. I now seeing what he was capable of doing I put my tail between my legs again and was back to square one with him.

The next month comes and my score has recalculated now and I'm way over the requirement so I do my best to avoid Johnson and get my promotion. The day comes before and Johnson pulls me in and ask why I think I should be a corporal. I give him some motivated speech about bettering the corps, teaching junior Marines, and fed him all the Marine Corps Kool-Aid I had. Luckily he bought it and told me I'm getting promoted. I'm stoked as hell and turns out Thor is about to get promoted again with me to. It was great till the first came. I was in line with everyone else and the first sergeant comes out and again tells me he doesn't have a warrant. I gave him a look like what the hell? He shrugs and tells me to fuck off esssitantly. I go back in formation and watch Thor and a few other guys get promoted.

At this point I'm the last of all my friends to get promoted. It kind of sucks when your lower rank then your friends you can't act the same at work. You have to set an example for the younger guys and do the whole military thing with discipline and respect. I let my frustration about my lack of promotion be known. They tell me for 3 weeks there working on it. Then I learnt about the Request Mast form.

When a Marine Request mast he basically is formally skipping everyone in his chain of command and going to the officers who

is in charge of him. You can go as low as you platoon officer or you could go as high as the first General in your command. I walk into the office where Johnson and my platoon officer work and sit down with the paper work. Johnson ask me if he could go talk to the first sergeant about this before I submit it. I tell him to go for it. He comes back with the first Sergeant in literally 2 minutes. He ask me if I would be willing to wait 30 minutes. I tell him I will but I'm going to start filling it out and if everything goes good ill shred it. I shit you not this bastard comes back in 25 minutes with my warrant and has everyone in formation and I'm promoted. I learnt that day those request mast forms don't play any games and when you have a legit issue everyone starts to actually work. When I get promoted I decide to have Johnson and Thor do the ceremony of putting the new rank on my collar. It was kind of a fuck you to Johnson. But Thor having been in the Marines a lot longer then me he had taught me everything I knew at that point in my career and made me a better Marine overall. At the end of the day it was Official I was a Corporal of Marines. One thing I noticed right away was the pay it was a nice pay bump and decided I deserved something nice
At this point I had the truck for a while now and at the time it cost me about 120 bucks to fill it up and was losing its fun factor. I just got promoted but I was losing interest in the

vehicle. Then I figured why not start spending my corporal money. I went to an exhaust shop and put the baddest muffler system they had on it the thing roared like a lion. My new hobby became going on the highway and there is about a 2-mile long tunnel. I would go late as fuck in the night and completely stop in the middle of the tunnel and floor it all the way through. It sounded beastly as fuck in the tunnels and I loved it again for awhile.

A few more weeks go by and I decided I wanted to bump. I went to the number one audio store in Hawaii and told them flat out I want my shit to be heard from a mile away. I gave them a price range of about 4 grand and they go to work. They rigged up 2 12's underneath the seat and replaced all the speakers with some dope ass high quality speakers. When I left I turned it all the way up till I got to the gate. The gate guard on base threatened to give me a ticket but I was so high on having my truck all modded up I couldn't care less.

When I pull up to the barracks parking lot I see everyone outside by the beer garden. This place is like a little outside area where we are supposed to drink beer but since it was always hot we only came out there in the cooler months. I see a bunch of guys I know and pull right up next to them and show off the sound system. Since there little portable speaker died I just played music from my truck.

What happened next was my first time using my Corporal Powers and badass truck to take advantage of some female boots. Two of these girls show up and everyone is chatting them up. This one girl asks who owns the badass truck and I trying not to be smug but say it's "mine". Then I had a jimmy neutron brain blast idea. The subs I had were directly beneath the rear seats and were facing up. When you put the seat down in the back and sit on it you will feel the vibration. I have these two girls sit in the back of my truck. I then go through my phone and put lollipop by lil Wayne. When the base hit I literally saw these girls legs start shaking and they got the orgasm face. I let the song finished and to say these girls were ready for some dick is an understatement. At first I try and take both of them back to my room and then one of the guys that was partying down there I think his name was Brandon comes next to us. I barely knew this guy but I figured it would be selfish to hog all the pussy. We end up going back to these girls room and for some reason I was in the mood to eat her out. I get her off and then I railed the shit out of this girl. I guess my testerone was super high because I was going for like2 hours. When the other two finished they just rolled over and was watching us fuck like it was a movie. I'm pretty sure I gave this girl the best dick she had ever gotten. Wasn't really saying much because I think she was like 19 but I felt like a complete badass. But being the badass I was your boy needed some sleep so I was out like a light when I was done.

I woke up the next morning and saw both of the PFCs were not as attractive as I though they were the night before. I decided it was best to bounce. I completely left the other dude there and went back to my barracks room. I checked my truck was good and the guy I left in charge of locking it up didn't disappoint me. I went into my room on my high horse and there I saw Tony looking really upset. He told me him and Khole was done with. When two people you're really close friends with split up it's like being a kid in the middle of a divorce. You want to support both but they bash the other one so much it makes it rough. I tried my best to be mutual toward both but luckily for me I was taking a little trip to the big island.

Chapter 12-Pohakuloa Training Area

My first trip to PTA was by far the best one. I went there three times but my first time was by far the most eventful. I flew in to the big island and it's such a complete different scenery compared to Oahu. The only way I can describe it is like country side with some dried up lava and huge. It was so beautiful coming in.

When I came in I headed up to the training area. The training area is toward the top of the mountain. This mountain is huge I think its almost as tall as Everest. Either way it takes us about 2 hours of driving basically straight up to reach our location. Being a motor transport mechanic we got a lot of special privileges out there. For example since for that exercise they had to bring up about 200 plus tactical vehicles that are really pieces of shit I got to ride around in a Tahoe to get my stuff up. While everyone else is in these hot ass slow vehicles I have nice A/C and a radio to listen to.

But when we get to the top is when the fun begins. I get partned up with one of the wrecker drivers Thomas. First let me tell you about the wreckers. Out of all the military vehicles they are the only ones that are actually bad ass. These trucks are like supped up monster tow trucks on steroids. Out of all the trucks I have been in the MK15 was the only military truck I genuinely would ride in all day it had A/C, backup cameras, cigarette charger ports, and was actually comfortable like a normal car. To drive one of these beast ass trucks though it is a special school you have to go to for a few months. Thomas was probably one of if not the best wrecker truck operators in Hawaii at the time. Paired with me we was the best driver/mechanic combo for the 2 months we was there.

We get situated and get the wrecker ready to help anyone whose truck can't make it up the mountain from the ports. The wrecker got brought up like 2 weeks before any of us got there somehow. But every single other truck was down at the port and getting matched up with drivers. Thomas and me get our radio set up and are waiting for a call. About 30 minutes into the convey up the mountain we get called and its time to roll out. We came in hot to say the least. The Mk15 weighs in about 100,000 pounds, has 10 wheels, and is about 20 feet tall.

Coming down the mountain Thomas had this thing going about 100 mph. On our way down we passed a few cars and I'm pretty sure they all shit them self's. We make it down and I see this truck completely smoked out.

I get out and see coolant everywhere it blew a radiator line. We go and hook this thing up on the side of the highway. We get a lot of looks from the locals and pretty sure the cars we passed saw us because they were mean mugging super hard. We get it hooked up and head back up. While the wrecker was a beast pulling an armored Humvee up a mountain it took a lot longer and couldn't hit a hundred up hill. We go and drop off the truck in the dirt lot where we all the trucks were suppose to be. Then we get the call to the A frame.

The A frame is the halfway point up the mountain. Since it was about 2 days of driving to get all the gear up the mountain Thomas and me went to the A frame that night to be ready in the morning. The A frame has this huge A wooden statue and a lot big enough for a bunch of conveys to stop at and take a break. Thomas and me wake up the next morning and was there for about 3 hours. We got really bored and decided to take the towing chains out and bust the rust. We hooked them up to the rear of the truck and drove around for about 30 minutes doing donuts in the truck. Then we got a call for a truck that was just outside the base on top of the mountain. Us forgetting about the chains head up and about 5 miles in a car pulls up next to us. At first we thought they was trying to race so we took off. But up hill most cars are faster then the 100,000-pound truck. It takes us a solid minute to realize what they are saying but eventually we realized. Most people would pull over on the side of the road. Not Thomas and me we had the biggest vehicle on the road by at least 4 times we hopped out and threw them back in the container. Once we finally get to the truck I see the problem. This was a 7 ton and its center wheel was turned completely left. Since it was only like 2 miles away and hooking up the 7 ton to lift the middle of the truck up was a bitch I had an idea. I whipped out the duct tape and had wrapped the arm that keeps the tire straight back to the frame. I was underneath this truck and while they had it moving I kept wrapping it up which in turned made it straighten out. Once the tire was straight I wrapped the rest of the roll on the arm and sent them on there way. They made it to the loading area without a problem.

The first few days of any field op is the worst. Getting set up is such a time consuming process and everyone is retarded and makes 2 minute ordeals into hours. But sure enough we get the maintenance tent set up, the portable work areas set up, and get unpacked a bit. But being mechanics while everyone else starts to relax we go to work. Since we had broke ass trucks get hauled up the mountain we had to start fixing them.
It was three of us Homes, Sherlock, and myself. The first thing we fixed was the 7 ton I duct tapped back together. Luckily when you go on these training exercises you spend a lot of time preparing. We had a storage container and was basically given a blank check to order any parts and bring out thWe literally brought everything from as big as an engine to light bulbs. The funny thing is while out there we used damn near everything we brought.

When we went to look at the truck that blew the radiator line we discovered the head gasket is blown. Repairing a head gasket is a job that requires a lot of precision and not something you want to conduct outside. But swapping the engine was totally something we could do outside. We strip this truck down removing the hood and everything in the way to the motor. Using the beast ass MK15's crane we yank this bitch out. Taking it out was fairly easy but putting it in was damn near impossible. When installing an engine you use a very specific lift that has alot of playroom and can be adjusted a lot. This crane was literally meant to just pull flipped over trucks out of shit so it wasn't very fine tuned. But luckily Thomas finessed the crane and after about 2 hours of struggling to get this thing set in it matches up and pops in like a puzzle piece. I get all the main components back on except the hood and the exhaust pipe. At this time it was pretty late like 10pm and everyone was in their tents sleeping. All of us Motor T mechs decided we needed to check it and ensure it worked. I fire up this thing and its just straight headers and lout as fuck. I then decided I should road test it. I Baja this thing over to the tent area it's a lot with a bunch of rocks so I start doing the nastiest donuts and burnouts. One of the guys came out to bitch but as soon as he got close to me I flipped it around and drove off. He was butt hurt but he was the same rank as me so I told him to fuck off. We then all proceeded to take turn "test driving it".

Goats you probably don't think there is a lot of them in Hawaii. The big island though is especially over populated with them where our training area is. The problem is when we do our gun ranges they get hit a lot and suffer since they just get hit via collateral damage. They also tend to jump out in front of our trucks a lot. There is a working party that deals with this issue. We are a couple weeks into the field op and the SNCO of our platoon comes out to where we are and tells me to grab my flak, Kevlar, rifle, and all my magazines and get ready to load up. I at first figure I'm about to do something stupid. About thirty minutes go by and a Humvee comes by and picks me up. I see a few other guys and start making small talk none of them know what we are doing either.

We get over to where all the helicopters are staged and we get out of the Humvee. We are directed over to a table where this Sgt is standing with a shit ton of ammo. He hands us the bandoliers full of boxes of ammo and tells us to load up all our magazines fully. I load up 180 rounds and still have about another hundred I put in my pockets. Then I see a helicopter land. Then one of the crew chiefs came out and gave us a quick class about how to conduct ourselves in a helicopter and got us all rigged up so we was dummy corded to the thing. I'm still confused as to what the hell am I doing, I ask the guy "hey you know what the hell we are doing?" The dude grins as we get loaded up and as the helicopter fires up He goes "your taking care of the goat problem". I look at my rifle and get the happiest look on my face. We head up in the air and it was amazing seeing the view. We could see the whole island there was no clouds out at all that day. Then they opened up the back end of the chopper and they started to descend a bit. The first guy lines up and the crew chief points at a heard of like 5 goats. The Marine opens up and starts firing on those bastards. He put it in burst mode and was having the time of his life. After watching a few of these guys I start to get really hyped up. Finally it is my turn I come up the platform load up my rifle and there I see a group of about 3. I throw that bitch on burst and light there asses up. They dropped immediately. We come around and it felt like seconds but I managed to dump all my rounds and went back to my seat in what felt like a minute. I was loading up all my extra rounds I had in my pocket and saw one of the Marines drop his Magazine out the helicopter the crew chief laughed his ass off and screamed to us "don't do that its littering". I made extra sure to ensure I didn't lose mine. I come back up and this time I'm dropping rounds and toward the end I see a heard of like 5 goats I go to light there asses up and I got all of them with not a round to spare. At the end of the day I got like 10 goats. We fly back to where we landed. We got off loaded and we are all like school girls giddy as hell. We clean up all the brass out of the helicopter and head back.

I get back to our base camp. I tell everyone about the greatest work detail anyone has ever done. I don't know if they still do that anymore. I haven't heard of anyone else doing it since I did but that was probably the coolest thing I had ever got to do in the military though.

While we managed to have fun up in that mountain there was one thing that sucked ass. The day my phone got ran over. One day we got a call two trucks were down. Thomas and me loaded up and then the other wrecker was right behind us. We get ready to leave and I notice his hood isn't latched. I tell Thomas to stop and I hope out and go latch it for them real quick. Being in the rush I didn't realize my phone fell out of my pocket. At the time I had one of those otter boxes on it. But when a 100,000-pound vehicle goes over it not much can be done for it. I realize it is missing as soon as we get to these "broken trucks". I literally plugged a wire back in and both of them ran perfectly. But we was trapped in between to ranges and couldn't leave. I use Thomas phone and start calling it and somehow it manages to ring. I get an answer it was some female I couldn't make out her name all I hear is her say specialist, which is an Army rank. We get back and I tell my superiors about my situation. At this point

Thomas and me had already made a great name for you so when I asked if I could go to every Army base they said go for it. I stop at the first one, which was part of a chow hall. I walk right into there Sergeant Major office and Army guys are chill as hell he had everyone under him at that base stop what they were doing and hit up everyone they knew on the island to see if they had my phone. Long story short they did not.

I'm on to the next one. While the first base was like teddy bear army people the next one was exact opposite. These guys were some hardcore Ranger dudes that had some badass shit. I drive up to there base camp and ask the soldier at the front about my phone situation. He tells me to hang tight and the Commander will come talk to mew soon. About 30 minutes go by and this beast of a man comes over. Looks like brock lesnar. He is gear queer to the max he had his ear muff walkie talkie, all the attachments on his rifle, and had a scar across his face. Not going to lie dude was a bit intimidating. But sure enough guy was nice as hell. I tell them it was a female soldier. He takes me to where the only two females he has under him are located which is the medic tent. He ask them and they reply no. I give him Thomas number in case he hears anything. What the dude did next cracks me up to this day. He looks at the number and goes "Why don't you just give me your bases radio frequency I can have it over there before a text message sends". This dude was being serious as hell I give it to him and my call sign and we head back.

I get back and go to talk to my superiors they tell me that by the end of the week they will let me go down into the city and go to a Verizon and get a new one. I appreciated there efforts but when in the field there is certain activities that need a phone and I just went cold turkey. A few days go by and I'm having phone withdrawals and all the first world problems. The officer in charge of my company comes back to me from the chow hall. He told me while grabbing food he was in front of some female soldiers and figured what the hell why not ask them. Sure enough they ended up knowing the girl who had it. Now the otter box didn't completely protect it. But for getting ran over by a 100,000 pounds it stood up quite okay. But by the time I got it the battery was dead and the charging port was toast. Later that week though we needed to get "truck parts" from an orileys was our excuse to leave the training area. I went down to Verizon and dropped like 500 bucks on a new phone. At the time I didn't regret it one little bit.

Toward the end they ask who wants to stay down the mountain and be at the port for 2 weeks and who wants to go home. The port is where the have the ships come and load up all the trucks and gear. But we only had one ship so it would take a day to get loaded. Then for it to go back and get off loaded was another day so we had a day off from loading it. The port obviously was right next to the water and was a dope set up. There was a small shack and some outdoor showers, a is storage container with surf boards and every water activity you could iAnd there was a little town within walking distance of it. The last thing, which was my favorite, was this old lady and her retired husbands who was a Marine would come all the time and make us Peanut butter and jelly sandwiches. Now your probably thinking so what its just PB&J. But I swear on my dead goldfish these were the best PB&J sandwiches you will ever have guaranteed. Another reason I wanted to stay was since I got a new phone I got on the tinder and had been chatting this island girl up who lived in the bigger city right up the road Kona and had already made moves to smash. I ended up getting to stay and was happy as hell.

Working at the port is probably the chilliest time in the Marine Corps. Your pretty much beach bums and for me since the beach shack was packed with to many people I set up a hammock in between two trucks. I woke up in the morning and the guys who also had hammocks around me would all grab some beers shotgun like 2 and go load trucks up on the ship. We spent usually from 7am to about 2pm doing this and then the ship would leave. After that we would go shower change into beach clothes swim in the ocean for a bit, jump off the docks, and play some football. When it started to get later we headed to Kona.

Going to Kona was about a 20 minute drive for us. We went to this place every other day for a week straight called Laverne's. It was chill as hell the servers and bartenders were all nice as hell and hot. They would hook us up with drinks since the typical crowd was retirees seeing young people really livened up the place. Now what I discovered after the second time going there was the girl I have been talking to work at the red lobster right behind Laverne's. I told her about it and she ended up coming over when she got off work. We end up talking for a bit and next thing you know we are in her car and beating cheeks. I honestly can't even remember her name but we did that at least 4 or 5 more times. She was pretty cute though I remember but pretty shallow.

Our final day of being beach bums comes and we are all pretty upset to be going back to Oahu. We go to Laverne's one last time before we leave and they are all sad to se us go. We get to the airport and are off back to Kbay. As soon as we got back to base I knew we was back to good ol Marine Corps life I got yelled at almost immediately for my hair. I forgot to mention the whole two months at PTA I did not have anything with a razor touch my hair and in the Marine Corps world I might as well have been Satan himself for that sin. Either way I go to the barbershop and had my mane cut and start to adjust back to the reality of my life.

Chapter 13-Getting out the bricks

The barracks we lived in aboard MCBH was one of the oldest and least habitable. The only one that was even worse than our was were the infantry guys stayed. Every weekend for about 2 months in the middle of summer they would do "maintenance" which consisted of having absolutely no Power in the barracks. What does that make you do? Well when it's about 85 degrees with 100 percent humidity shit got hot real quick. Me and a guy named Aaron started a new tradition go home with girls who had AC. It at first seemed pretty difficult but we had a pretty good record actually. The funny part was when we was real desperate we would go home with some beat ugly chicks and then "pass out" on their couch just so we didn't have to put out. One of my favorite ones those was my weekend with Steve.

We wake up one morning to sweaty pillows and all the lights not working. I take a cold shower in complete darkness and Tony somehow was out for the count. I got outside and see Steve on the walkway. I ask him if he wants to go out somewhere and he said sure. The only problem was he was still 20 at the time. I knew of only one bar that would probably not Id him at 9am it is the most legendary bar on the island located in Kailua this establishment is called Porky's.

We head over there and sure enough they serve him a beer no Id we are set. We are sitting there and not to sure how old they thought we was but fairly odd parents was playing on the TV. At the time we didn't care we had AC, place to charge our phones, and beer. Then good old momma san came out. This lady had the biggest crush on me. She worked at the bar and since it was just us 2 in there she started taking shots with us. Then she kind of hustled me.

She made a bet if I could beat her at a game of pool she would take me into the back and let me do whatever I want and if she won I would buy her a few shots. She straight up destroyed my ass without missing a single shot. I ended up dropping like 100 bucks on shots. The time goes by throughout the day and we were there for over 12 hours and drinking the whole time. Night time comes around and this is where it starts to get blurry. I somehow got momma san to take me in the back and after we got done having black out drunken sex I come out and Steve is gone. For some reason he ended up leaving and went to some house right down the street. I magically appear at the right house and door is wide open. I come in and he is sitting on a couch. I look at him confused as hell and get him to come back with me. This whole time I never saw anyone else in the house. We get back to Porky's and get in my truck. I decide since I'm super annihilated I will just park at the Safeway next to base and sleep it off. I get to the Safeway parking lot and close my eyes. I open them back up again and I'm in my barracks room in my bed. I immediately freak out and ensure all my stuff is there and it was. I go check the truck it's parked no damage.

I go to Steve's room and there he is sleeping. Turns out I somehow in a miracle drove on base made it to the barracks and went to sleep. Steve somehow went on his own adventure to Kahunas got drunk. Ended up having a conversation with a palm tree and one of the guys on duty carried him to bed. Luckily for me though that was my life changing moment and I felt like such a piece of shit for literally not having any idea I was driving that I vowed to never drive drunk again. Luckily I have been able to hold myself to it ever since.
While Honolulu is cool and the place you think of when you hear Hawaii. Kailua will always be my favorite place. For the longest time Tony had given me shit for my only tattoo and said only

bad Asses get the ribs done. At the time Jägermeister was my favorite liquor of choice and told him if he drafted up a design I would get it put on my ribs. He lit up happy as hell and Tony was actually a really good artist he spent about 2 weeks drawing it and it looked sick as hell when he was done. Tony had already gotten a few tattoos since we been there we went to his guy and set me up with his guy Kelvin. He was pretty dam good. One Saturday no AC we figure lets go get this shit started. I was thinking it couldn't be that much more painful then my arm. Tony told me I should get something to eat and drink before we went. I said I was good but boy was I wrong. I get there and god damn that shit hurt. I had to take a break every couple hours it was no joke. The dude was getting a bit upset but I was literally white as a ghost. 8 hours later I get the outline finished. I decided I would do the shading a later date. A couple weeks go by and I go and call Kelvin up and no answer on his cell phone. I stop by the shop and talk to one of the guys there. Apparently about a week after he started my tattoo dude over dosed on opiates and died. I was pretty bummed out who was going to finish my tattoo? No one did and to remember old Kelvin I still have just the outline.

When we merged shops I met a dude named Rakiem. He was a big buff black dude who was gay. He was my first gay friend and turns out gay dudes know how to get dimes chicks/dudes. Rakiem and I friendship really started when we was working late and just started getting drunk after 1630 and till we went home and avoiding the superiors. He was telling me about all these clubs I have never heard of. Apparently the gay scene on Hawaii is popping, didn't know that but it was a thing. Anyway he tells me I need to change up my wardrobe and he will take me shopping when the weekend comes. I figure why not I could use some new clothes. The weekend comes and we head over to the mall in Honolulu. We get to express and I literally felt like I was on that show about the gay dudes and the straight guy getting him new clothes. I ended up walking out of that Express store with quite a bit of clothes for the amount I spent. Rakiems boyfriend had a buddy or something who was a manager, basically hooked it up. We go back to the barracks and he tells me we are going out to Honolulu tonight and the pregame starts now. We go get a bunch of beers and start drinking. I get dressed I'm in this blue button up shirt that was tight as hell on me and some jeans that felt like my balls were being cupped. We get down to this place and its right next to the zoo in Honolulu. I can't remember what it's called but they have a bunch of gay flags but the music was bumping. We go up in there and all of these guys literally started drooling like a dog over us. I finally knew how it felt to be an attractive woman and damn it felt good. The best part was I told all of them right away I was straight and they didn't care. I was talking to this pilot for Delta and he was telling me about all the places he has taken his guy friends.

Not only that the guy was actually pretty cool. I try and hook rakiem up with him but he wasn't having it. As the night goes on I'm having a great time getting drinks bought for me and great conversations I almost started to see what the hype about being gay was until I saw the only woman there.

Now there is a lot of dimes in the world but this Russian girl was a damn dollar. She was literally perfection. Perfect from the head to her toes. Luckily for me I was the only straight man around her so no competition. She was dancing by herself so I go up and start dancing with her. We hit it off and she tells me about herself and I'm literally shocked someone this attractive is talking to me. I make my move to make out with her and shit worked flawlessly. I started feeling her up and next thing you know we are outside. We was behind this big ass tree and she starts sucking my dick. Then out of nowhere some people walked up and she got scared she said "oh shit that's my boyfriend" and she ran away. I'm pretty sure that the people wasn't her boyfriend but regardless I never saw her again. Blue balls and one Coors light away from being black out drunk I go back and find Rakiem. He is with some dude and tells me we are going back to this guy's hotel room. I couldn't care less I just wanted to go to sleep. We head back into this guys hotel and I immediately drop right on the bed and was out. Rakiem was definitely doing gay stuff in the bed next to me but I wasn't awake for any of it. The thing that really scared the shit out of me was when I woke up. I woke up early as hell to take a piss and the only person there was the gay dude. Rakiem was nowhere to be found. Not only that but my phone and wallet were gone. One thing I never lose no matter how drunk I get is my wallet, keys, and phone. I was still completely dressed so I walked out of there like a ninja. I get down to the street and looking like a hot mess I walk into a Jamba juice. I'm sitting there and remember I had a recall roster in my shoe. A recall roster is a little piece of paper with everyone you work with phone numbers. That shit was my savior today. I go to the girl working at the register and she lets me borrow her phone. I call Rakiem up and luckily he took all my stuff just in case the dude was trying to rob me. I asked why not just take me to and he didn't have a real good answer for that. Beside the point after I curse at him for a good minute he comes and picks me up. Coming back home after a long night of drinking and just being a hot mess taking a shower and going into your own bed is the best feeling ever.

Chapter 14- Thor's Bachelor party

I have never thrown a bachelor party or even participated in one at this point in my life. All I knew was what I've seen in the hangover. I literally attempted to plan a night just like that. It was 4th of July weekend and Thor was going home right after the holiday to get married. Since none of us was going I decided we should throw him a bachelor party. This is where I learned winging it was the way to go. July 3rd I start making calls to all the hotels in Honolulu trying to find one and they are all booked. Michael and me said fuck it lets drive down to Honolulu and go hotel-to-hotel see if there was any last minute cancellations.

On Waikiki beach all the hotels are damn near touching each other so going to each one isn't that hard. We started at the Trump hotel and walked to each one and they said we are full until we got to the Halekulani. This was the most expensive hotel in Waikiki and when Michael and I walked up to the front desk and asked for a room this smug ass douche barely would even look at us. He scoffed and said, "yes we have a room but I doubt it's in your guys price range". I look at this asshole and say, "try me bud how much?" He replies again still not even looking at me "750 a night". Now I've never really had the need to flex on anyone but this dude really pissed me off. I stand there completely silent and it took this dude literally 2 minutes before he looked at me. I stared him right into the eyes and said "yea let me get it for the weekend boy". He rolled his eyes at me kind of in disbelief. He runs the card and I think he was expecting it to decline but it didn't and I told him I would be back shortly to valet my vehicle. When Michael and I came down we was in his little Malibu I decided I really wanted to flex on that hotel receptionist so I went and got my truck. When we head back to base we tell Steve about the plan and to get Thor down there by 9pm. Michael and I pack some clothes and stop by the liquor store on base and get everything.

We head back and pull into the hotel parking lot. The valet guy goes to get in my truck and I tell him no I want that douche at the front desk to park it. He looks at me weird as hell and calls the manager over. The manager explains to me douche isn't qualified to be driving peoples car. I give the hotel manager a bullshit story about how he was so nice I wanted him to do something so I can tip him. The manager said "oh well I can have him bring your stuff up to your room for you". I smile and said "oh that would be great". The douche bag comes over looking mad as hell. I stood there smiling while standing next to my truck go "oh hello again please be careful with my items I doubt you could afford to replace them". He started turning red as he grabbed our bags out of my truck and just trying to push this guy's buttons I go" don't drag them out the back I couldn't imagine having to repair the seats". This guy turns red as a tomato as he finished pulling everything out. Michael and me are just giggling like schoolgirls at this point. He goes to lead us to the room. He opens the door up for us and damn this was probably the nicest hotel room I've been into at this point. When you're paying 700 plus a night you get everything from slippers to robes and damn it was nice. The guy takes all of our stuff off the cart and he literally had his hand out and wouldn't look at me. I walk over with a beer in my hand and wait for him to look at me. I told him "see what happens when you judge?" He remains silent and I start chuckling and go okay this could have gone differently but be like that. I was going to give him a 50 if he would have just been a man and apologized for being a douche but since he wanted to stick to his douche ways I handed him a crumbled up one dollar bill out of my pocket and slammed the door in his face fuck that guy. I always try to be nice to people in hospitality but when you are just flat out smug and judgmental because of someone's appearance ill go 0 to 100 real quick and go in debt just to prove a point.

After we take our pictures of the amazing view we get to work. We had until 9pm till Thor got there and it was 3pm. We had to get dinner reservations, strippers, drinking games, and all the other bachelor party items. Luckily it being 4th of July weekend getting a couple of strippers only took 2 phone calls and 300 dollars. Check in the box on that we are good. The second was getting dinner reservations. The coolest restaurant in Hawaii is called top of Waikiki its this skyscraper bar that spins in a circle boojie as hell. I call them to make reservations for 5 plus and sure enough they had one opening for 11pm fucking A.

Next getting beer bongs and shot glasses. In Waikiki luckily they have two things hotels and dam ABC liquor stores every 100 feet. Michael went and got all the stuff we needed. We literally thought of doing a bachelor party at noon and had everything ready by 5 pm. Not going to lie was pretty proud of ourselves getting all this done in less then a few hours. Michael and I thought to reward us by getting a head start on our drinking. We changed into those bath robes and no homo watched the sunset on the patio of the hotel drinking cheap ass liquor with rockstar energy drinks. Rockstars and red bull are the only things that go me through that night.

Steve lets us know they are all on the way. I go to confirm the strippers and it aligned up perfectly. Thor would be here for about 45 minutes before the strippers. Just enough time to get him liquored up. Thor walks through the door and we already had all our cheap plastic shot glasses full ready to go. He was a good sport we ran him through the gauntlet he had to individually take a shot with all of us and we had like 5 guys there. When we finished the shots we all shot gunned a beer. Then we get a knock on the door. It was the "police" and two girls came in with their handcuffs and put Thor in the chair. They started dancing on him pouring beer all over him and making him take shots off them. I never had strippers come to me but it was actually a good time they were really nice and not trashy or anything. Way classier then typical strippers I have encountered. We do that for about hour and a half and they wrap it up. The best part was at the end the strippers security guard lady gave us some cards and said if we wanted some extra money they are hiring male strippers. I looked into it, for every bachelorette party they do there are about 20 guy shows they do and I wasn't about it.

We all started to get ready for dinner. We walk our way into the lobby all beers in hand and I see my favorite front desk hotel employee. He gave me a stank eye and I smiled and waved. As we are walking to the restaurant we stop and see the fireworks and they were cool but they literally do it every weekend so it wasn't that big of a deal for us just kept people in our way.

As we get up to the restaurant and sit down it gets brought to my attention 3 of the guys are only 20. I remembered I still had my fake ID in my wallet. We have them spread out through the table as far away as possible. As the waiter is coming around taking our orders and checking IDs we start sliding my old fake id under the table. Somehow this lady either didn't give a shit or was dumb it worked perfectly. I told them it wouldn't work at the real bars and they said its fine they were going to take a taxi back to base afterwards. We get our drinks coming and since it was Thor's party they hooked it up. This is the type of place that chargers 12 bucks for a shot we ended up all getting at least 5 or 6 drinks and food. The most someone payed was like 100 bucks which for this place is pretty damn cheap. The trippest part about this place is the spinning. Where the actual floor where you sit spins. When you walk to use the restroom for obvious reasons it doesn't spin. Walking back after 10 minutes your table is on the complete other side. I walked around freaking out until luckily my waitress took me back to the table. Apparently I wasn't the first to get lost two of the other guys laughed about it. We wrap up and pay our checks and decide since we are dressed up we should go to Rum fire.

Just like everywhere else we have gone so far this is best of the best. Rum fire is litty and we ended up talking to some girls there. We wasn't really trying to bring them back to the hotel just more of the lines of talking to them. They were really hot and figured there was no way they do one night stands anyway so I just started fucking with them saying they weren't even that attractive and should have tried harder. After about roasting these girls for 10 minutes somehow don't remember perfectly I guessed it turned there sadistic asses on. Next thing you know I take them to the side of the pool and they start making out with each other. I'm watching this in complete disbelief and I start to join in. It was about the coolest few seconds of my life.

What happened next I still kick myself in the ass to this day? I was making out with these chicks for no less then 10 seconds. Then all the cheap liquor, energy drinks, fancy liquor, and beer decided it wanted out. I felt it in my stomach coming and I turn my head right into the pool and I hurled about 7 hours of binge drinking right into the pool. I look back up and the two girls are gone and replaced with this big ass security guard he was a local and what that means is he gets his kicks by beating the shit out of military guys. I was drunk but knew damn well I was about to get my ass beat. I rolled me eyes at him and I booked it. I yell for Thor and the other guys and high tailed it out the door. I look behind me and this dude is right on my ass like a freight train. I see a wall and a palm tree up ahead. Later Thor told me that wall was like ten feet high. I made the choice to jump over the wall and hopefully loose this guy. I leapt up and grabbed the palm tree and swing my legs over the wall. I don't remember much about where I went from there but I later on I went back and I swear there was no way I made it over that wall but Thor insisted that I did.

I don't know what happened in between if we made phone calls or what but after we all scattered from rum fire going our separate ways to lose security we end up outside Moose's. We have a couple drinks there dancing and last call goes we go to the hotdog stand outside. Those hotdog stands next to bars have to make as much if not more then the bars I love them. Walking back we end up meeting some well I don't really know a better word but hookers. Only problem was they didn't disclose that upon bringing them back to the room.

We get back to the room and it was just Thor and me everyone else decided to go to Kelly O'Neil's since it was open another couple hours. Thor and I hatch up a game plan trying to be suave with it and put the moves on. It worked obviously and Thor took his into the bathroom and I was in the bedroom. It was pretty boring fuck she was one of those skinny girls that are use to the guy doing all the work. But I just ran away from the giant and been drinking for almost 12 hours at that point I was the dead fish. I manage to get my nut and when the other girl came out we started walking them downstairs. They tell us we need to give them 500 bucks to get home. I sobered up real quick and go "da fuck you live japan?" They argue with us for a bit we are telling them pretty much we don't have 500 bucks to give them. They threaten us that there pimp is going to come and collect.

We laugh at them and pretty much tell them to fuck off were going to bed. Apparently after we went to sleep the hotel security earned their paycheck that night. Some guy was down in the lobby for 2 hours trying to find us. The hotel security had to subdue the guy and he ended up in jail. Luckily those dumb bitches didn't know our names or anything about us. Morale of the story don't fuck with hookers there not it.

Around noon the next day we all manage to rise from the dead with sore legs and hangovers that could take down the Hulk. We all shot gunned a beer and head down to the pool. I'm sitting in one of the lawn chairs bathrobe and sunglasses on straight chilling. Guess who comes to my side the best front desk receptionist on the planet. I knew something was up because he was smiling and actually looking at me. He ask me if I could come talk to the manager real quick. I have an idea already where this is going. I walk over to the lobby and the manager pulls me in to a back office. The guy then explains we had several complaints over the last night and that the night crew had to call the police due to my "visitors". Long story short I got kicked out the hotel. Butt hurt as hell I gather everyone up. We get my truck loaded up and on my way back to kbay I freeze my credit card I already knew they was going to try and hit me with all the bullshit charges. Sure enough they tried to charge me additional 4 grand but my bank navy federal was the real MVPs and shot it all down. We get back to kbay thinking the weekend is over until my buddy Ryan tells me about the camping trip there about to go on.

The camping trip is pretty much the part 2 of that weekend. Up until this point I haven't really talked much about legit barracks rats. These barracks rats are the females that get tossed around the barracks and fuck pretty much every dude they can. Our barracks rat name was Jessica and no I did not fuck her came close but even I had some standards and when you've had sex with as many people as her that just isn't it coach. This camping trip consisted of about 7 guys and 2 girl's one of them being the barracks rat.

We get up to where the camping area is and its starts off as a pretty innocent camping trip. We are playing football, fishing, eating hotdogs, and burgers. Then it all changed when the sun went down. About 4 beers in the barracks rat was on one. She started groping me and usually I would go with it but I just watched her do the same thing to pretty much everyone else there. As the sun goes down we start a bonfire and start making some smores and drinking beers. The night goes on and as we get drunk our beer supply dwindles. Where we was camping at there was a Safeway about 2 miles down the road. A couple of us load up in my truck and head out of the camping grounds. We drive by an open field and the yee yee redkneck in me takes over and I conduct multiple donuts in the field kicking up all the dirt. After we get back to the task at hand we get to the front and the camp has a gate closed and locked up. Pissed as hell we head back and inform everyone. Somehow an unopened bottle of tequila gets brought out and we start taking shots. That thing about tequila and clothes coming off turns out is a real thing. About 2 shots in on the tequila this barracks rat is naked and swimming in the cold ass beach by our camp site. At first we are kind of in disbelief. Then not going to say names three guys go in there with her. I'm not too sure what happened in the water but after awhile they come back. There was a tent right by the fire and 2 guys went in and with the barracks rat. They start running the train on her and it was pretty funny at first but about 5 minutes in shit just went from being funny to kind of weird. Thor and I said fuck it and were going to walk to the store and grab beer.

We start walking and make it about a few hundred yard pass where the locked gate is. I look over to the other side of the road and I see some horses. I look at Thor and smile, he tells me not to do it but I'm on a mission. I wiggle through the wire fence and walk toward a horse. I pet him for a few minutes making sure he trusts me and is calm. At this point in my life Thor and me have 1. Had no idea how to ride one 2. No idea how to get on one without a saddle. I go and try and swing my leg over this bareback horse and let me tell you it looks a lot easier in the movies. My first attempt I jump up and smack my stomach on his side and slide right off. Now with the wind knocked out of me I stare at the horse. I was lucky as hell it didn't kick me and run off I think it felt bad for me because it just stood there. Thor tried to convince me to just give up on the idea.

I try one more time jumping as high as I can I get my stomach on his back and swing my legs over, I got it! I sit up right on him and look down at Thor smiling like a motherfucker. He keeps trying to get me off but is trying to not get the horse upset. I'm sitting there on top of him and I realize. I have no idea how the fuck to ride a horse! I try kicking him on the side but I guess my feet were upfront too much because he didn't do anything. I'm sitting there confused as hell and Thor finally convinces me to get off the horse. I should have probably broken every bone in my body that night or got syphilis but someone was looking out for me.

Thor and I walk back to the camp and the two guys were done running a train on the barracks rat. They are sitting by the fire and not to long after another guy comes out the tent. I ask him if he did her as well? He did not seem to have as much fun getting the sloppy thirds. As the night is winding down I decide that I was going to sleep in the bed of my truck. I walk over there and use a beer box as a pillow I lay down and all I hear is someone dry heaving. I look over and see Khole and Tony right next to my truck and she has been throwing up since the tequila got brought out apparently. Tony was pretty pissed because even though they were broke up he still got stuck baby-sitting her. I feel kind of bad so after she got her shit together I let them have the bed of my truck. I walk back over to the camp and everyone is sleeping I sat down by the fire and I see Jessica come out the tent. I talk to her for a bit and she convinces me to go swimming with her. I strip down and we both head into the ocean. It felt pretty good being out there then I made a move on her. I go in to start kissing her she pushes me away. At first I was thinking to keep trying to pursue her but I don't know if it was the cold water sobering me up or what. I realized she just got a train ran on her had been used and most likely had some sort of STD. I decided for my health it was good I passed that up. I walk back to the bonfire now just white smoke decide to start packing everything up.

When everyone woke up finally, I had everything loaded up and ready to go. It had been a long weekend and I was ready to go home. We start driving and on the way home I pulled over like 5 times to watch everyone throw up. I think I must have drank myself sober that weekend I was perfectly fine. We get back to base and a few days go by and turns out the barracks rat gave all of those guys syphilis. I had never been happier not to have sex. After that weekend I took it down a few notches.

Chapter 15-going away's

I haven't really talked much on serious topics for the majority of this because it just doesn't make for good Stories. One thing no one ever tells you about being in the military is seeing people leave. While in your 4 years of active duty you see a lot of people leave. The people you spend day in day out with. Going through some of the roughest times of your life. Being there for the best moments of your life. The people you serve with literally become closer than your family. Most of your friends in the military are going back home to some state your try and say you're going to visit eventually but never do. With social media it is a little bit better now but for the most part your never going to see these people again. You take them to the airport and talk about your plan to meet up in a few months and drop them off. As time goes by though you start to get a lot tougher and not as emotional.

Sam was the first person I was truly close with that I watched leave. He had mentored me and gave me the idea of what a good Marine should be. The day he left we went to his favorite restaurant it was a bunch of us. We talked and had a bunch of plans to meet up with him when he gets settled into Washington DC. When we wrapped up dinner we all went to the airport and paid for parking. We watched him get his bags checked in and it was a very emotional moment for all of us as we watched him head through security. I ended bumping into him years later in San Diego but beside that haven't really seen him since that day.

Thor who I spent 2 years living with. He taught me basically everything I know about being a mechanic. Was quite literally a big brother to me. Had made me a better Marine and man overall. His going away went something like this. His last day we drank some beers at the beach and his friends flew in to party with him in Hawaii for his last week. I saw him for maybe a couple hours the last week. All of his friends flew out the day before him. The morning of his flight I asked him if he had everything and was ready. He loaded up his suitcase and I drove him to the airport. I dropped him off at the terminal said "later dude" he got out and quite literally haven't seen him or talked to him since.

Now while watching a lot of people leave sucks its not always bad. Watching people you dislike leave is quite fun. When the guy in charge of the tools left I was happy as hell. He had been a douche to me for the whole time he had been there. Till the end though since I had a truck and he had dogs, wife, kid, and a whole bunch of shit. He asked me to take him to the airport and I hesitated at first. I told him he had to fill my tank. The night before he was set to leave I was at like half a tank I drove my truck around all night till the gas light came on. I go and pick him up the next day and head immediately to the gas station. At this time I think gas was like 4 bucks a gallon. This dude ended up spending like 120 bucks filling up my tank.

I go and drop him off at the main terminal after he gets his dogs and there crate out someone tells him he has to take them somewhere like 2 miles down the road. I really wanted to be a dick to him and make him figure that shit out. But then this weird thing called my conscious hit me and I saw his wife and kid. I get all the info and I ended up dropping his dogs off at the place and tell him. He obviously was grateful. But best believe if that dude didn't have a wife and kid I would have left his ass stranded there.

The hardest going away though without a doubt was mine. At 3 years I had seen a lot of people come and go and there was only one person that remained. Tony even if I didn't mention his name he was there for just about every single moment in Hawaii. I had never developed more of a bond with anyone then him.

My finally week Tony and I kind of started to distance ourselves. The room that we had lived together in for the last 3 years became inhabitable. The floor literally started to leak water out of it. The facility manager told us we had to move. I had the military movers coming in three days so I basically said "I'm not fucking leaving". Tony on the other hand had a few more months so he obviously had to move rooms. I would come into work and since I was leaving soon I didn't really have time to work much so Tony picked up a lot of slack and was busy as hell during the day to where I didn't really get a chance to talk to him.

Friday afternoon I flew out so I had one more wing night. I went into kahunas and everyone was there. I didn't get stupid drunk but had my usual back scratcher drink race. Tony gathered everyone around and they brought out my going away plaque.

Its one of my most prized possessions it is a flywheel painted blue and red with a write up that goes like "your time in combat logistics battalion 3 has been well appreciated. As for all of us here at motor t platoon it is time to say Farwell to a great Marine. We want to thank you for everything that you have done for us. From breaking trucks more than they already are to swapping motors in record breaking time. You have been an inspiration in so many ways we want to wish you nothing but the best in your future endeavors stay peachy beachy and Dathan let me tell you about this plaque shit its for the birds". At this point I have seen and presented god knows how many of these plaque to guys. But when it happens to you it a pretty emotional moment.

Usually your suppose to give some sort of speech but all I could muster up was "thanks guy I love you all". We finish up the night and I get back to my shitty condemned room. I double check all my stuff is packed and go to sleep.
I woke up the next morning and bring my suit case down to the barracks duty office and leave it with him for safe keeping. I go turn in my key to the room I have spent the last 3 years in and go pick up my plane tickets. I stop by the shop and say bye to everyone. I go into the changing room where Tony is. We look at

each other for a minute and hug each other real quick. I walked out of the building and didn't look back. I hoped into my friend's car that was taking me to the airport.

When leaving your unit let it be to another unit or to go back home it's hard. You have become a family with these people over the last few years. They know everything about you just like you know them. But what is the hard pill to swallow is knowing everyone else is going to keep the wheel spinning. No matter what rank, age, or what you did while there it keeps going. There is no real way to prepare for that but when leaving you have a lot of emotions going through you. Luckily for me I hit some Honolulu traffic on my way to the airport and was running behind. Instead of sitting in the airport having a drink thinking about my time in Hawaii I was rushing through the airport.

Chapter 16- Re-Enlisting

Staying in or getting out of the military is a process either way. The start to getting out or staying in begins about nine months prior to your EAS date sometimes even more. At a year from getting out I was all aboard the get out train and was more than ready to be done with the Marines. What I did though was submit a re-enlistment package just so I could tell the Marine Corps to shove it up there ass and get out of work for a bit to get papers signed. While in the process of doing this though there is only one side of it. When even considering staying in everyone above you pressures you because that's all they know. The people that mentor you and answer all your questions for the last three years are going to swear that staying in is the only correct action. After a while it starts to get in your head and you forget to realize all of the people who tell you getting out is bad, have never done it.

When going around with this folder of paperwork you start to get treated a lot better as well. The superiors who have been dicks to you for the last few years all of a sudden become real nice. Those weekend duty's go to some other guy. Then they write the recommendations for you. For the first time in your military career you're getting hyped up. The people who have been saying you suck ass for the last few years go on to write about how you are basically the greatest thing since sliced bread.

One saying that Marines who stay in is "don't judge the Marine Corps over this unit". Which is some bullshit career Marines do is talk about how shitty the present unit is and how the last unit they came from was amazing. Truth of the matter is its all the same shit just wrapped in different paper. Problem is after hearing it over and over from different people you start to buy into it. You tell yourself "yea your right it's just this unit the whole Marine Corps isn't this bad". Now there is nothing wrong with staying in the military for 20 plus years. I think the way it works people who are on the fence end up getting pushed one way because there is no devils advocate. While its not necessarily always a bad to stay in the military the problem is it back fires when you get the guy who should have gotten out stays in. Now believe it or not there are some Marines who are above average, some in the middle, and some below average. I like to think at that point in my career I was on the upper level of average. Now back in the height of the war they needed everyone that was capable to stay in. they offered money, duty stations prefences, and a bunch of other monetary values to get people to stay in. Now that the guy who was way below average stayed in because he got 20 grand is now in charge of 40 plus Marines. Deep down all these guys cares about themselves. Its easy to spot these guys because they don't know there jobs, they come in after their Marines are already been at work for hours, and they leave work before anyone else there selfish managers who use there Marines as pawns.

The issues with that are the smarter Marines who are above average, the ones that have really great ideas and ways for improvement see that and want change get out. Its very frustrating because the ones who are trying to make it a better place get shot down because the shit bags below average are in charge don't want change because the system is set up for them. They want it to stay the same so they can weasel their way into a retirement pension with little to no effort. But for every weasel there is one role model. The guy who stayed in because he loves the Marine Corps for what it is and not what it gives him. For me it was who else but Johnson. Out of everyone in the unit he actually got out for two years. He was the only

person that Enlighted me to the full spectrum and said something along the lines of. Put in the re-enlistment package and go home. Think about it hard and then do it again. Flip a coin and whatever side it comes up on you'll know what you want. I hadn't gone home in awhile so I took his advice got my 800 dollar plane tickets and when home for 4 weeks.
I get home and see my family. They are all happy to see me. When your home for longer than 2 weeks you start to get pretty bored. I started to remember why I left my home town another point to re enlisting. I went to a few mechanic shops and I ended up at dealership. The service tech manager was a really cool guy. Showed me around the shop but it was different, there was no music, everyone was on their vehicle just working. It paid pretty well and the guys all had pretty good sense of humor would have got along with them great but something seemed off.

The thing that I believe what sealed the deal was seeing my high school friends. If you have been reading all of this you have seen a lot has happened to me over the last 4 years. I had been places most people dream of visiting. I had met people from all around the world. The amount of women I have slept with has been pretty exceptional. Experiences I have had you could never pay for and all of that was 100 percent credit to the Marine Corps.

Would you like to know what my high school friends have been doing for the last four years? Every single one of them have not moved out of the bedroom they had in high school. Every single one had dropped out of community college. None of them had a car worth more than 3 grand. All of them worked at the same franchise restaurant and not been promoted. They also have not left town once in the 3 plus years I have been gone.
What's really weird about the military is while you're gone you have life changing experiences and when you come back home nothing changes. It's really odd at first and makes no sense how no one else has had significant life changing events it's been a couple years. That's where it really kicked in for me. If I got out I would end up just like my high school friends. Sitting back in my old bedroom maybe doing school. But most likely working a bare minimum job at some franchise. Talking about doing something big but never really going through with it. That shit hit me in the core and I knew what I had to do. I flipped the coin and Johnson was right I already knew what I had to do. I picked heads for staying in tails for getting out. I looked at it but

couldn't tell you for the life of me what it landed on. I was staying in.

From there it seemed like everything just fell into motion. A few days later the person in charge of submitting re-enlistment packages called me. He informed me it came back approved and needed an answer to give to his superiors on what I wanted to do. I told him I wanted to do it and would sign it as soon as I got back. I went and had a beer with my dad that night and told him about my plan. It was pretty funny how supportive he was I think it was just because how much of a bum my brother became and he didn't want the same for me.

I fly back to Hawaii and get settled back into my barracks room. I at this point have not really told any of my friends about my choice. The funny thing was between Bruce, Tony, and me I was the only one staying in. Truth be told they were both way better Marines then me at that time and if you had to pick one of us I would have been last.

When re-enlisting I got one incentive which was duty station preference. What that means is you get to literally hand pick the unit you want to go to. I knew a few things I did not want to go to Okinawa. Went their once and sucked so badly it wasn't even worth mentioning in this book. There was no way in hell I wanted to go back to North Carolina. I never had been to California but always wanted to go. The biggest base in California is Camp Pendleton I start looking up all the units over there and see a few that looked nice. Camp Pendleton also is about 30-45 minute drive to San Diego. Someone informed me about a place called MCAS Miramar. It was literally in the city limits of San Diego and was a straight Air wing base.

At this point in my career all I have heard about the wing is how relax it is and chill and little to any work. Coming from a logistics battalion where you work 10 hour days more then you don't it sounded like the perfect vacation. Go live in San Diego chill out meet some Cali girls. I look up some units there and I find one called Marine Wing Communication Squadron 38. I thought to myself there couldn't possibly be much for a truck mechanic in an air wing communication unit.

I go back to the guy who is charge of submitting my re-enlistment paperwork. I give him the unit and it all lined up perfectly they had one spot just open up. Seemed like everything was going perfectly.

I get my papers and all I need is an officer to sign and give me the oath and a staff non-commission officer to witness it. I go back to my office and sit down at my desk and look at my paperwork and realize this is it. I walk over to my officer's desk and ask him if he would do the honors. He agreed and said all I had to do was go find a Staff Sergeant or above to participate. I walked out into hallways and see Staff Sergeant ball. I tell him the chief warrant officer needs to see him. He groans and heads over.

We both walk in and chief warrant officer is standing next to his desk. Ssgt ball kind of knew what was going on so he just walked and stood right next to the officer. I march in front of them. Ssgt Ball reads the first paper "I hearby honorable discharge Corporal Dathan Beach from the United States Marine Corps on this 15th day in October 2015 Signed Patrick M Tucker Lieutenant Colonel United States Marine Corps commanding". I sit there for a few seconds and chief warrant officer ask "is there's anything I want to do as a civilian for the next 10 seconds" in a jokingly manner. I reply "nah I'm good Eric". We all laugh a bit and Ssgt Ball reads the second paper "this certificate herby declares Corporal Dathan Beach has been accepted for re-enlistment in the United States Marine Corps on this 15th day of October 2015 signed

Patrick M tucker Lieutenant Colonel United States Marine Corps commanding"

Then with all seriousness the Chief warrant Officer looked me dead in the eyes and said, "Lift your right hand and repeat after me"

I (state your full name) do solemnly swear that I will support and defend the Constitution of the United States against all enemies, foreign and domestic that I will bear true faith and allegiance to the same and that I will obey the orders of the President of the United States and the orders of the officers appointed over me, according to regulations and the Uniform Code of Military Justice. So help me God."

I repeated it after him. He shook my hand and said congrats you did it.

I just re-enlisted for four more years.

Manufactured by Amazon.ca
Bolton, ON